Hell Come Calling

Big Jim Wolfe rode into the town of Greasewood wanting nothing more than a hot meal and a good night's sleep but instead found himself defending a family of Mexican sheep-herders against a power-hungry cattle baron.

With a crew of hired guns backing him, Jack Whelan had the town totally under his control and was ready to launch an all out bloodbath in order to gain the rest of the valley. But the one thing he hadn't counted on was the deep-seated sense of right and wrong that Jim Wolfe lived by. He wasn't a man to go looking for trouble, but he certainly wouldn't walk away from it. . . .

By the same author

Death on the Devil's Highway

Hell Come Calling

Josh Lockwood

A Black Horse Western

ROBERT HALE · LONDON

First published in Great Britain 2012

ISBN 978-0-7198-0582-0

Robert Hale Limited
Clerkenwell House
Clerkenwell Green
London EC1R 0HT

www.halebooks.com

Typeset by
Derek Doyle & Associates, Shaw Heath
Printed and bound in Great Britain by
CPI Antony Rowe, Chippenham and Eastbourne

CHAPTER ONE

Everything around the settlement of Greasewood was the color of dust devils and dried blood.

It sat like a heel blister at the head of a summer-dried valley angling away to the northwest, and big Jim Wolfe rode into it slowly, in no kind of mood for stupid games.

His back ached from riding; he wanted a bath and some clean clothes, maybe a hot meal and a good night's sleep, but a large knot of people gathered in the street was blocking his way.

He reined in at the edge of the crowd, wiped a work-hardened hand over the stubble of his beard and scanned the ragged group in front of him.

'What the hell's going on?' he asked a lanky cowhand standing near his stirrup.

'One of Jack Whelan's men working a woman over,' the man droned. He turned away quickly after he spoke, rising on his tiptoes to get a better view.

Jim clamped his teeth hard together at the answer

and felt the coppery taste of anger rising in his throat.

Working a woman over?

There was something totally wrong with that picture.

Without another word he nudged the grulla mare into the throng of people to witness the action for himself.

What he saw made his blood boil.

The guy in the center of the crowd was squat and powerful, built like a Rocky Mountain grizzly, his hat tugged low over his eyes, shading him from the relentless sun, and he had a crooked grin smeared across his face.

The woman he held up by a fistful of hair appeared to be Mexican, though it was hard to tell right then. Her cheeks were swollen and red from the repeated slapping he was giving her, her eyes were puffed shut from the beating, and a rivulet of blood leaked from the corners of her mouth.

Even as Jim watched, the man raised his beefy right hand, whipped it down against her cheek, and a spray of blood from her nose and split lips spattered out on to the dust.

'Bitch!' the man bellowed. 'I told you what would happen, didn't I?'

Not one person in that ragged crowd of people made a move to stop him.

Except for big Jim Wolfe.

He leaned down on his saddle horn, slid the heavy

Colt Peacemaker out of its holster, and leveled it at the grizzly across his forearm.

'Do that again, mister,' he said over the low babbling of the crowd, 'and I'll put one through your ear.'

The grizzly glanced up, narrowing his eyes. 'Who the hell are you?'

'Nobody,' Jim replied evenly. 'Just passing through.'

'Then keep on riding. This don't concern you.'

The metallic clicks of the Colt's hammer being thumbed back sounded overly loud in the dry desert air and a sudden hush fell over the crowd of onlookers.

'It does now.'

The grizzly snorted loudly at his words, slammed his heavy hand down against the woman's face one more time, and Jim pulled the trigger.

The slug took the grizzly in the temple, erupting blood and bone and brains out the other side of his head, and snapped him sideways as if he were a puppet on a string.

He sprawled into the dust of the street on his belly and didn't move again.

The good citizens of Greasewood went suddenly wide-eyed, mouths dropping open in shock, and they began edging away from him in groups of two and three. The fear etched in their eyes was painfully obvious to him and it made no sense.

The beaten woman stood tottering on trembling

legs for a few seconds, then started wilting toward the dust of the rutted street. Another woman – this one obviously Mexican – rushed forward from the dwindling crowd and grabbed her.

Jim swung down quickly from his worn saddle, ground-hitched the mare, and scooped the battered woman up in his arms as if she were a child. She couldn't have weighed more than a sack of oats.

'Is there a sawbones in town?'

'Sawbones?' The woman's forehead furrowed in a frown at his question.

'A doctor. Is there a doctor in town?'

'*Sí*,' she said with a nod. 'Doctor Morales. Just down the street.'

'Good enough,' he muttered. 'Show me where.'

'Miguel,' she murmured to a slender boy standing behind her, 'bring the horse.' She turned silently then and started away.

'You know her?' Jim asked.

'My younger sister, *señor*. Miguel is our little brother. I don't know how to thank you for stepping in.' Her ebony hair swayed with her movement and her skirts made a faint rustling sound.

'No thanks necessary, miss, but I'm a little surprised no one else tried to stop it.'

She leveled her eyes at him as they walked, as if trying to find an insult in his words.

'I tried,' she croaked. 'He slapped me once and the others held me back from attacking him again.'

She hesitated in the street for a moment then and

swept her hand up toward the covered boardwalk. 'That's Doctor Morales on the walkway.'

Jim lifted his eyes to the gaunt-faced Mexican standing in the shade of the false-fronted buildings; he felt surprised and relieved at the same time. The doctor wore a pressed white shirt with the sleeves rolled up, open at the collar, a neatly trimmed grey beard, and had years of hard-earned experience etched on his face.

'My God, Corazón,' the doctor rasped, 'I saw the whole thing. Come in. Come in.'

He held the door to his office open and bobbed his head to Jim. 'Please, *señor,* just lay her on the table there, and thank you so much for helping. You are a brave man.'

The office was shadowed, surprisingly cool inside. A sturdy mahogany table stood prominently in the center of the room, a stack of folded white towels at one end of a long counter, and an array of brown bottles lining the shelves on both sides of the space.

The doctor picked one of the towels off the neat pile, dipped it in a basin of cold water, and handed it to the beaten woman's older sister.

'Hold this against her cheeks, Corazón,' he said softly. 'It will help reduce the swelling while I clean her up.'

'Your name is Corazón?' Jim asked after the aging doctor had stepped away.

'Yes,' she said with the hint of a smile touching her lips. 'Corazón Alvarado.'

'And your sister?'

'Juanita.'

Juanita's eyes blinked open at hearing her name spoken but she appeared to be woozy and let them slide slowly shut again.

'Not that it's any of my business,' Jim ventured, 'but what was that all about out there?'

Corazón shrugged her softly rounded shoulders and turned her attention back to her sister. 'This man, this Jack Whelan, said something inappropriate to her as she passed by and she insulted him. He does not forgive insults.'

'Was that him slapping her?'

'Oh, no,' she murmured. 'That was one of his hired guns. He has many of them working for him and everyone in the valley lives in fear.'

He studied her for a long moment then, noting the care she used in dabbing at her kid sister's face, the softness in the blackness of her eyes. It spoke volumes about her character and he liked what he saw.

He'd known a few women like her before. Steady, purposeful, but it was a rare thing in these parts. Most women were worn to a frazzle by the time they got this far west. The prairie, the desert, had a way of taking the starch out of them.

In a real quick hurry.

'You live in the valley?'

She looked up again and nodded. 'Yes. We graze sheep north of town, but it's not a life you'd wish on your worst enemy.'

'I can believe that,' he said. 'Cattlemen don't like mutton-punchers much.'

'Is that what they call us?'

'Among other things,' he muttered. 'They say sheep kill the open range because they eat grass all the way down to the roots, pollute the water holes, and carry scab mites.'

She nodded her understanding, dipped the towel in the basin of water again, and continued dabbing at her sister's cheeks.

'That's probably true for the sheepmen who don't take care of their flocks . . . there are many coming north from Sonora and Chihuahua . . . but we are not among them. Our animals are well kept and free of disease.'

He cocked his head at her response. 'I'm guessing the cattlemen can't tell that by looking.'

'Not many people can.'

Doctor Morales stepped back to the table at that moment and began carefully wiping the dried blood from Juanita's nostrils.

'At least her nose isn't broken,' he uttered softly. 'I count that as a minor miracle.'

'She'll be OK then?' Jim asked.

The doctor pressed his lips together and nodded. 'She'll be fine, *señor*. She is young and full of life. Likely she will have a headache for a time but I can give her some chamisa tea for that. The swelling will go down in a day or so and the lips will heal by themselves.'

Jim wagged his head, still amazed at the brutality of the man he'd shot. 'Damn,' he mumbled, 'after all the hoorah out there in the street, I could use a drink.'

'And I'd be happy to buy you one,' the doctor offered. 'The saloon is just there, across the way.'

They all heard the heavy thud of boots on the walkway and turned in time to see a slight, lantern-jawed man step in through the open door.

He was trouble on two legs: accustomed to giving orders, accustomed to being obeyed, and Jim knew it the minute he laid eyes on him.

There was one in every town.

'I'm Jack Whelan,' he rumbled, fixing Jim with hooded eyes. 'Maybe you've heard of me?'

'Not that I can recall.'

Whelan wasn't happy with the answer. 'Well, I *have* heard of you, mister. My boys tell me you're the one they call Wolf, without an "e", and they tell me you're right handy with a gun.'

'I get by.'

Whelan nodded curtly, his face a mask of grimness. 'Just so we understand each other, Mister Wolf without an "e", I run this valley, this town, and I want you out of it. Whatever you came here for, get it done quick and move on.'

Jim met his look evenly; there was no trace of humor in his voice.

'If your men know anything at all about me they would have told you that I don't take orders very well.'

Whelan huffed at his statement. 'You might live to regret those words. Then again, you might not.'

'I don't take threats very well, either.'

'I want no trouble in here, gentlemen,' Doctor Morales interrupted. 'This is a place of healing, not bloodshed.'

'And there's no need for further bloodshed,' Whelan added, still peering at Jim. 'You just do what you came for and trail on out. Be a lot less painful.'

'For who?' Jim asked quietly.

Whelan huffed again and spun on his heel. 'You've been warned,' he growled over his shoulder.

They watched him walk away without speaking for a long moment, then turned back into the office.

'I'm afraid you've made yourself an enemy, *señor*,' the doctor said. 'A very ruthless enemy.'

'It's not the first time.'

He wiped the sweatband of his battered hat with his ragged blue bandanna, set it back on his head, and glanced up.

'You said something about buying me a drink?'

Corazón Alvarado stepped to the open door, hands planted on the flare of her hips, and peered at the man's broad back as he and Doctor Morales paced toward the saloon across the street.

So that was Wolf. The man they called Lobo down in Sonoita.

Remarkable.

He must stand over six feet tall with his boots off,

had the frostiest blue eyes she had ever seen, and brown hair that curled over the collar of his shirt like the tail feathers of a Shanghai rooster.

He had shoulders an axe-handle wide, fists like tempered steel trip-hammers, and wore his gun tied down.

It was well known in Sonora that the man didn't go around looking for trouble . . . but he wouldn't walk away from it, either.

Trouble just naturally had a way of finding him.

He was just what this valley needed.

He was almost a legend south of the border; she had heard the story of him taking apart the Cuchillo Loco gang many, many times.

Cuchillo Loco had been a half-breed Yaqui running with a bunch of *pistoleros* from the Sierra Madre Mountains. They had raided the town of Sonoita every summer for as long as anyone could remember. Gold and horses had been their favorite things to steal but, on occasion, they had also pilfered the scarce corn crop and cattle. Once in a while they had even kidnapped young women who were never heard of again.

God only knew what happened to the women, and no one in the village had nerve enough to ask.

It was told that this gringo, this man they called Lobo, had ridden into town in the middle of one of their raids, didn't like what he saw, and got into a set-to with one of Cuchillo's men.

The war that followed, they said, lasted two bloody

weeks with Lobo gunning Cuchillo's men down one and two at a time – some of them running for their lives. The battle finally ended when Cuchillo himself came at Lobo with his knife.

The story was that Lobo emptied his gun into the half-breed's heart, tied his body over a scrawny burro, and sent him back to the mountains.

Now, remembering how easily he'd taken down the man who'd beaten Juanita in the street, it was easy enough to believe.

CHAPTER TWO

The whiskey burned like a branding-iron going down and took Jim's breath away for a second. He wiped his mouth on the back of his fist, set the glass down on the scarred counter, and caught the barkeep's eyes.

'I'll have another.'

'You ain't real popular in here, mister,' the slope-shouldered bartender mumbled, leaning both elbows down on the counter. 'If'n I was you, I'd drink up and be on my way.'

'Just fill the glass.'

'You see those gents at the end of the bar eye-ballin' you?' The barkeep mouthed the words just loud enough for only Jim and the doctor to hear.

'I see them.'

'Them're some of Whelan's men. They get tanked up, there's liable to be some shootin' in here.'

'I'll keep it in mind.'

'Just sayin', is all.'

'I got your drift the first time around,' Jim replied. He pointed a blunt finger at his glass and continued. 'If you're antsy about pouring for us, you can just leave the bottle and we'll take care of ourselves.'

The bartender made a dubious face, poured another shot in their glasses, left the bottle, and ambled away.

The place was crowded for a Saturday afternoon, the only light coming from a couple of kerosene lanterns hanging over the bar. A pall of greyish smoke hung like a shroud near the ceiling. The mirror behind the bar was streaked with dust but made the row of brown and green bottles lined up along its base look twice as wide.

'He's right, you know?' Morales said quietly. 'You gunned down one of their friends a while ago and they'll be looking for some payback.'

Jim threw down the second shot of raw frontier whiskey then turned toward the aging doctor and asked the question that had been plaguing him ever since Whelan had stormed into the doctor's tiny office.

'How'd Whelan get this kind of power?'

Morales shrugged. 'It's common knowledge,' he mumbled. 'He controls the water. A few years back he dammed up the creek on his place and, without water for their stock, the ranchers downstream were forced to sell out.'

'They didn't fight back?'

'Not against all the hired guns Whelan had taken

on. He got their land and stock dirt cheap and now owns almost the entire valley.'

Jim nodded his understanding and asked the next obvious question. 'How'd the Alvarados hold out?'

'They have a spring on their place. It's not very big, you know, but enough for their flock. In the summer they take the sheep to the high meadows where there is always water. Whelan can't control that.'

'That was a gutsy thing you did out there, mister,' a wiry man leaning down on the bar next to Jim piped in.

Jim cocked his head at the man's statement and turned.

'The right thing, anyway,' he replied. 'I don't know if I'd call it gutsy.'

'Well, I would,' the man said, half under his breath. 'Not many men in these parts would go up against Whelan's outfit. I'm Hoot Rafferty, run the livery stable, and I've been around here long enough to know.'

'Livery stable? I wasn't sure there was one in this town.'

'There is,' Rafferty said. 'Just down the street.'

'Good to know. I'll probably be bringing my mare in there after a bit.'

'Be glad for the business,' the hostler ventured. 'Ain't been getting much lately.'

'Whelan's doing?' Jim asked.

Rafferty lifted his hands in uncertainty. 'That'd be my guess. He doesn't remember me, but we were in the same outfit during the war . . . the Fourteenth Brooklyn Zouaves.'

'Yankee, hunh?'

'Yeah, but that don't make me any less of a man.'

'Never thought it did,' Jim said, tipping another shot of whiskey into his glass. 'You the guys wearing the baggy red trousers?'

Hoot nodded somberly. 'Yep, that was us.'

'Easy targets.'

'That's the way Whelan felt about it, too.'

Hoot took another swig of the fiery frontier whiskey and leveled his eyes at Jim.

'Damned good bunch of guys. I guess we were in just about every major battle there was in the East, you know? Bull Run, Antietam Creek, Fredericksburg, Chancellorsville. We sort of got paired up with the Sixth Wisconsin, and at Gettysburg it was our two regiments that stopped you Rebs from taking Cemetery Ridge.'

Jim wagged his head. 'I heard that was some serious damned fighting.'

'It was that,' Hoot said with a faraway look touching his eyes. 'Hand to hand, by God. Bayonets and clubbed muskets and no quarter given.'

'Damn,' Jim mumbled.

'And Whelan was all right in there, you know? Did his part and no one had any complaints. Then they marched us south into what they were calling the Wilderness, and it was there that he showed his true colors.'

'You lost me on that one, Hoot.'

Rafferty squinted at him and lowered his voice. 'You happen to notice that headband he wears?'

Jim shook his head and the scrappy hostler went on. 'Yeah, well, he cut and ran at the battle of Spotsylvania Court House. They found him hiding in the brush about a mile back of the line and brought him in that afternoon.

'He was branded for a coward – a capital "C" burned right in the middle of his forehead, and they kicked his ass out of camp while the regimental band played the Rogue's March.

'He never forgave them for it. Wears that headband to cover up the mark they gave him. Fools most men, I guess, but I know better.'

'And what's all that have to do with me?'

The liveryman cocked his head. 'The man carries a terrible grudge. When the war was over he went hunting the people who did that to him, you know?

'Colonel Johnson was the first one he did in. Him who pronounced sentence. They say he caught the colonel coming down the road from the surrender at Appomattox and blew his face off with a shotgun. Captain Boudreaux was next. He was the one who cut the buttons and facings off Whelan's coat. Hung him from a tree in his own front yard, he did. Got Sergeant Striker, too. About three years ago over in Santa Fe, the way I heard it.'

'And?'

'And I'd say you got off on his bad side, snuffing

out one of his men like he was a tallow candle. Like I said, the man carries a terrible grudge.'

'Sounds to me like he's about two bricks short of a load.'

'You got that part right. Anyway, I've got to run. I'll be at the stables when you're ready to bring your horse down. End of the street. You can't miss it.'

Rafferty tossed off the last of his whiskey, clunked the glass down on the counter, and marched out.

'I've got to roll out of here, too,' Jim said quietly.

'Yes,' Morales answered. 'I should get back to my patient, but there's not much more I can do for her right now.'

'You think a shot of laudanum would help?'

The doctor shook his head. 'It'd be much too strong for her. I'll make her as comfortable as possible in the back of their buckboard and tell little Miguel not to hit too many bumps on the way back home.'

They finished their drinks, strolled slowly out the door, and crossed the dusty street together.

'Maybe I'll see you again, Doc,' Jim said, offering his hand.

'I'd like that. You're welcome anytime.'

'Good enough. You take care.'

Jim unwrapped the reins from the doctor's hitching rail and walked the grulla to the end of the street, where gritty Hoot Rafferty was waiting for him in a rocker that had seen better days.

'Water and grain her and curry her down, Hoot,'

he mumbled handing the reins over to the hostler.

'I can do that,' Rafferty replied. 'Be four bits.'

'Any place in town to get a hot meal? I'm so tired of my own cooking it makes my nose bleed just to think about it.'

The hostler met his look evenly and jerked a thumb over his shoulder. 'The Cimarron Hotel is probably the best bet, but only if you're going to rent a room. Otherwise you can grab a bite at the saloon. Not very good grub but it sticks to a man's ribs.'

Jim recalled the jaundiced looks he'd been getting from the knot of Jack Whelan's men who'd been standing at the far end of the bar while they were there and shook his head.

'I reckon I'll take my chances at the hotel.'

'Right there across the street,' Hoot told him, nodding toward the door. 'The cook's name is Rosa. Just tell her I sent you and ask if she can warm up some leftovers.'

'Sounds like a plan to me,' Jim muttered. He dropped the coins into Rafferty's outstretched hand and ambled away.

The Cimarron Hotel was a two-story frame structure with the name painted in foot-tall black letters all the way across the false front and set slightly back from the street.

No one stood behind the counter when he pushed through the door and he followed the aroma of freshly baked biscuits down a narrow hall. The small dining room he walked into still had cups and dishes scattered across a long mahogany table and a heavy-set Mexican woman was busy picking them up.

'Hoot Rafferty sent me over,' he began. 'Said if I asked real nice you might warm me up some left-overs.'

'Are you a guest in the hotel, *señor*?'

'Will be as soon as I eat.'

She tilted her head slightly and studied him for a long minute. 'You're the one who saved Nita Alvarado in the street, aren't you?'

He shrugged. 'If that's what you want to call it.'

'I thought so,' she whispered. 'There'll be no left-overs for you, *señor*. For you I will make steak and eggs.'

She spun on her heel to return to the kitchen, then stopped and smiled at him over her shoulder. 'I am Rosa Reyes, *señor*, and you can count me as a friend.'

He grinned at her words. 'Seems like a man can't have too many friends.'

'Not in this town, anyway.'

'You got any coffee back there, Rosa?' he asked, nodding toward the kitchen door.

'Half a pot of Arbuckle's Best,' she answered. 'Do you take anything in it?'

He shook his head. 'Black is fine.'

'I'll bring you a cup.' She nodded and stepped on through the kitchen door.

He lowered himself to a hard-cushioned chair, legs akimbo, and pondered the events of the last few hours.

Seeing the woman getting slapped around in the street had stopped him in his tracks. He was no angel by any stretch of the imagination, but he did have a deeply ingrained sense of right and wrong. Something his pa had pounded into his head back in the Missouri breaks.

And the beating was just about as wrong as it could be.

The shooting had been a spur of the moment thing.

He hadn't even known the man, had nothing against him really. It was just the brutality he had shown in smacking the girl around.

The bastard had enjoyed it.

And then there was Corazón. She was everything a man could want in a woman. Everything *any* man could want and, from the way she'd warmed to him, it made him want to know more about her.

Rosa emerged from the kitchen again, set a heaped plate of food down in front of him and struck a hipshot pose at his side.

'Will you be with us long, *señor*?'

'Doubtful,' he answered. 'Just wanted a good night's sleep and a hot meal before I trailed on out of here.'

'That's too bad,' the cook said softly. 'This town has a great need for a man like you.'

Jim didn't respond. Realistically, there was nothing he could say.

He hadn't intended to raise any kind of ruckus

when he rode into Greasewood. It was a chance to cut the trail dust on his way West, nothing more, and he had wanted it to remain that way.

Now, because of the shooting, he was in it up to his eyeballs, had the whole Whelan bunch gunning for him, and knew in his heart that he couldn't walk away.

He ate slowly, savoring every bite of food, and watched the plump cook clear away the dishes.

He rented a room for the night on the hotel's second floor and, tired as he was, sleep wouldn't come. Instead, he sat at the window, through which came not a breath of air, gazing blankly at the dusty street below.

He was thinking about Corazón Alvarado.

The woman had eyes a man could drown in, hair like molten lava down to the middle of her back, and a way of walking that made her skirts rustle when she moved.

She made a man think about putting down roots, of leaving something more on the land than his reputation. The kind of woman a man would go to war over, then wish to hell he'd stayed home with her instead.

She was the kind of woman a man would be proud to have on his arm while strolling around the town plaza, and he tilted his head wondering if there were any chance at all she'd be interested in a down-at-the-heels drifter like him.

The thought plagued him.

He spotted the dark shadows of three men moving along the boardwalk half a block up the street and eased back away from the window. Their movements were a mite too furtive to his way of thinking, and the sight of them set off a well-honed instinct for survival.

It was just such instincts that kept a man alive out here.

The men stopped in the pale fan of lantern light leaking out the door of the general store, peering up toward his room, talking quietly among themselves.

The nearest one drew his six-shooter, thumbed open the loading gate to check the load, and slid it back into his holster.

Jim wagged his head sadly, knowing in advance what was coming; he pushed himself slowly erect and drew his own pistol from the gunbelt hanging on the lumpy bed's headboard.

It didn't have to be this way.

He'd righted a wrong when he rode into town, nothing more, nothing less, and it made no sense at all for these men to be hunting him.

Riding for the brand, they would call it. Whether it was above board or not.

Jack Whelan called the shots in Greasewood and they carried out his orders. All very simple and it wouldn't matter a damn to them that another man was supposed to die.

That was the name of the game in cattle country.

Jim shoved a pillow under the thin blanket over the bed to make it look as if he were sleeping and paced back to the hard cane chair by the window.

It wouldn't be long.

He heard the footfalls coming up the stairs, sounding hollowly in the hallway, and waited with the heavy Peacemaker balanced on his thigh.

Shadows blotted out the lantern light showing under the door for a brief moment, the knob turned but didn't open, then the door exploded inward under the force of a well-placed kick.

Two men crowded into the square of light at the same time; fanning their hammers back as fast as they could pull the triggers, they drilled shot after shot into the pillow he'd placed on the bed.

Wolfe clenched his teeth and fired at the bigger of the two.

The shot hit the man squarely in the chest, slammed him back against the wall, and he slid to the floor as if he were drunk.

Turning only slightly, Jim squeezed off another round, and watched grimly as the second gunman was also jerked backwards into the wall.

Jim stayed put a minute longer, waiting for the third man to make his play, but the echo of footsteps running back down the stairs told him the last bushwhacker had cut and run.

He pushed himself up and paced to the shattered door, the Peacemaker still at the ready in his hand. He scanned the hall for any more sign of trouble, then let his gaze settle on the gunmen he'd taken down.

Twin smears of blood stained the wall where the two had slid down. One still sat against the wall, his head lolled forward on his chest, the other had flopped over on his side. They were both very, very dead.

The acrid smell of gunpowder hung heavily in the air, the quiet after the storm of gunshots was almost overwhelming. Then, one by one, doors along the hallway cracked open.

'What happened?' a paunchy man in a grey nightshirt asked through a narrow opening. 'Where's the manager?'

'Right here,' another man cut in. 'What's going on?'

'You tell me,' Jim answered. 'These jokers kicked my door down and came in shooting.'

'Whelan's men,' the manager uttered. The words came out like a blasphemy, and Jim couldn't blame him.

The manager squinted one eye and peered at Jim through the other. 'You're going to have to pay for the damages.'

'No, I won't be paying for a damned thing,' Jim muttered. 'As a matter of fact, I'll be wanting my rent money back. I'd be safer sleeping in the goddamned stables.'

He turned back into the room, set his low-crowned hat on his head, strapped the gunbelt around his waist, and picked up his saddlebag. 'You can talk to Jack Whelan about the damages,' he said evenly.

He nodded toward the bodies still slouched against the wall and started out.

'You might ask him about a couple of caskets while you're at it.'

CHAPTER THREE

Jack Whelan tilted back in the heavy oak chair, boots up on the once white tablecloth, and folded his arms across his chest.

'So what's the upshot?' he rumbled to Jethro Hightower, the slack-jawed gunhand slouching just inside the door.

'Rafe and Curly Bob both bit the dust,' the hired gun drawled. 'Kicked that jasper's door down, went in with guns blazin', and he took 'em out like they was targets in some damned shootin' gallery.'

Whelan narrowed his eyes. 'And what did you do?'

'I backed the hell out of there. What did ya reckon I'd do? He still had four shots left in that Black-Eyed Susan of his and I wasn't quite ready to meet my maker.'

'Damn him!' Whelan blurted, slamming his fist down on the table. 'Who is this guy, anyway?'

'Hell come callin', from what I've heard,' the hardcase muttered. 'Got the reputation of bein' real bad medicine on both sides of the border and word on the street is he don't play around.'

Whelan glanced away, staring at the dust-hazy sunrise through the narrow dining-room window, and wagged his head. 'Why does everything have to be so damned complicated?'

'What d'ya mean, boss?'

Whelan lifted his hands in uncertainty. 'I don't know. This is a real sweet deal we've got here. No one to pester us, no law for miles around, we make our own rules, and it'll get even better once we drive the Alvarados out. This Wolf character can only mess it up.'

Hightower paced slowly around the table and poured himself a cup of coffee in one of Whelan's delicate porcelain teacups.

'What d'ya want to do about it?' he asked, his pinky finger suddenly jutting up in the air.

Whelan shrugged. 'I've got to think this one out, Jethro. You hang around the bunkhouse for a day or so, and I'll let you know. Nobody crosses Jack Whelan and just walks away from it. Nobody.'

He pressed his lips together for a moment and drummed his fingers on the tablecloth. 'What do we do with this guy?'

The gunman threw down the rest of his coffee with his pinky still thrust in the air, set the teacup down a little awkwardly, and paced toward the door.

'Whatever you figger out, boss, you know I'm good for it,' he said over his shoulder.

'We'll see,' Whelan replied flatly.

He waited until the door closed behind his long-time foreman and cupped his chin in the palm of his hand.

The Alvarados were a definite thorn in his side. They were only ones in the valley who had their own water, the only ones he couldn't push out of the way. The only ones standing between him and total domination of the valley, and he didn't like it.

If he could add their spread to his own, he'd be able to run maybe another 1,000 head of beef; he'd be far and away the biggest rancher on the Mogollon Plateau.

With the railroad pushing east from Los Angeles, that represented a sight of money. He'd be the only rancher in the area capable of supplying them with the kind of meat they'd need for the huge crews of engineers and Chinese coolie tracklayers who would be coming through.

Then, too, once the railroad was finished, there would be a flood of new emigrants coming West: those who didn't have the gumption to cross the prairies by wagon, and they would be a built-in market.

One way or another, the Alvarados had to go.

The old man, Pedro, was as stubborn as a Missouri mule and twice as cantankerous. Peace-loving by nature, he wouldn't fight back. Wouldn't even wear a gun, and that made some trumped-up gunfight with him almost out of the question.

No, it would have to be some other way.

This Wolf character had to go, too.

And he had to go first.

The unmistakable sound of a frying pan being clanged down on a cast-iron stove woke Jim and he glanced warily around the loft, surprised that the Colt was still in his hand and lying across his belly.

He pushed himself up from the deep pile of hay he'd been sleeping in and peered around yet again.

A trusting soul he was not.

Feeling safe after a moment, he slid the Peacemaker back into its holster, brushed the bits of hay off his clothes, and started down the ladder.

He caught Hoot Rafferty in the stable's tiny kitchen just as he was picking slices of bacon out of a black iron frying-pan. He nodded to him from the door.

'Still above ground, are you?' the liveryman asked quietly.

'Just barely, by God.'

'Gonna be hotter'n nickel night at a whorehouse today,' the hostler mumbled. 'You hungry?'

'I could eat.'

'Grab one of them plates then. Coffee's on the stove. Heard some shooting over toward the hotel last night and figured it was you.'

'Couple of Jack Whelan's men,' Jim said. 'Broke my door down and came in throwing lead all over the place.'

Hoot chuckled softly and bobbed his head. 'Yeah, and I hear tell they won't be throwing much more. Whelan ain't going to be too happy about that.'

'That's his problem.'

He accepted a plate of bacon and eggs from the hostler, poured himself a cup of hot, black coffee, and lowered himself to the long bench at the rough-sawn table.

'I'm taking it you don't have much use for the big bug?' he ventured.

'Not so's you'd notice,' Rafferty said around a mouthful of scrambled eggs. 'I was one of the guys who stuck it out at Spotsylvania, you know? A lot of good men died that day, and there that no-account sonofabitch was slinking around the brush with his tail between his legs, well out of harm's way. In my opinion he deserved everything he got. They should have hemped his ass right on the spot.'

'You don't mince any words, do you?'

'Not this week.'

Jim snorted at Hoot's declaration and leveled his eyes at him over the rim of his cup. 'We had our share of deserters, too.'

'Hell, I think everyone did.' Hoot nodded. 'But usually they headed for home after the battle. Not right in the middle of it when every man was needed.'

'That's true enough.'

Jim glanced toward the stable doors, sensing the heat that was already building over Greasewood.

'I was thinking about riding out to the Alvarado spread,' he said. 'Sort of wanted to see how the kid sister is doing.'

'Good idea,' the hostler replied. 'Being Mexicans, there's very few people in town give a good goddamn whether they live or die.'

Rafferty washed the mouthful of eggs down with a hefty swig of coffee and continued. 'Shouldn't be that way, but it is.'

'Damn shame, that,' Jim muttered. 'Near as I could tell they seemed like good people.'

'They are good people. Give you the shirt off their back and never fault you for needing it.'

'Where they located?'

Hoot tilted his head to the north. 'Ten, twelve miles out of town. Out along Kitchen Creek. Just follow the wagon track. You can't hardly miss it with all the bleating and baaing going on and that damned wet-dog stink of lanolin hanging in the air. Next to my wife's cooking, that's got to be the heaviest smell in the world.'

'Aw, come on, Hoot,' said Jim, holding back a belly laugh, 'your wife can't be that bad.'

'Oh, yeah?' the wiry hostler challenged. 'Why the hell you reckon I'm cooking my own breakfast down here in the stable? I swear that woman could burn water.'

Jim laughed at the liveryman's words and bobbed his head toward the chipped enamel plate in his hand. 'Well, there ain't nothing wrong with your cooking.'

'There's more if you want it, and the coffee's always on. You'll have to excuse me now. Got to get started on my work.'

Jim nodded his understanding and threw down the rest of his coffee. 'I'll be out of here in a few minutes.'

'Want me to saddle your mare for you?'

'I'll manage,' Jim replied. 'You just do what you have to do and I'll see you later.'

He rose to his full height, wandered back into the stables, and saddled up almost by rote.

'I left the dirty dish on the table, Hoot,' he said, leading the grulla out into the open.

'I'll get it. You watch your topknot out there, big guy. I doubt Whelan's men have forgotten about you.'

Jim stepped into the saddle and rode slowly north along the wide street, feeling the strange looks he was getting from the townsfolk as they swept the porches in front of their shops and scurried home from the general store. Looks that ranged from somewhere between awe and total disbelief.

By now he was sure they'd all heard of the shoot-out in the hotel and he couldn't blame them for their stares.

They didn't know what to make of him, whether he was some kind of knight errant who rode into town or just totally out of his mind. And it didn't bother him for a minute.

He picked up the wagon track that Hoot had mentioned on the outskirts of the settlement, nudged the grulla into a ground-eating canter, and scanned the countryside around him with a practiced eye.

The burned-out hills gave way to stands of pinyon pine a few miles north of town, just beyond a slight ridge in the valley floor; the air was filled with the raucous calls of blue jays, and buff-colored mule deer watched him cautiously from the dappled shadows under the trees.

Ahead of him the valley, narrow and summer-yellowed, opened on to a stretch of grassland studded with clumps of scrub oak and willow along a shallow creek that meandered down the middle.

He slowed the grulla to a walk, eyeing the steep slopes of mountains to the east and west and the small knots of white-faced cattle grazing quietly in the gathering heat.

It had the look of good cattle country, plenty of water, widespread stands of grama grass, and he could well imagine why Jack Whelan sought control of it.

It could make a man rich.

If it didn't kill him first.

The Alvarado ranch house was a low adobe structure with strings of red peppers dangling from rafter poles and drying in the never-ending high desert sun. Another adobe off to the side looked as if it could have been a shearing shed. The yard was a patchwork of pens made of woven ocotillo ribs.

Hoot Rafferty had been right. The rancid smell of lanolin hanging in the air was almost overpowering.

A black-and-white Border collie with floppy, butterscotch ears and one blue eye barked from the porch as Jim rode into the yard, then scampered out to greet him with his tail wagging in greeting.

'How you doing, pooch?' Jim murmured, swinging down from the saddle. He crouched down in front of the little bundle of fur, grabbed a fistful of cheek hair in each hand and scratched the mutt behind both ears.

He glanced up just as Corazón stepped through the front door. She wore a chocolate brown skirt, a spotless white blouse, and looked like a million bucks.

'She must like you,' she said softly, coming down the steps. 'Normally she doesn't take to strangers.'

He didn't respond, just stood up watching her approach.

'I was hoping you'd ride out,' she said. 'We don't get many visitors.'

'Well, I wasn't winning any popularity contests in town.'

'I'd offer you some breakfast,' she said, 'but we're just getting ready to move our flock to the high meadows. You're welcome to ride along if you'd like and I'll cook you something special when we get there.'

He nodded at the offer. 'I never rode herd on a flock of sheep before.'

'Nothing to it,' she said softly, nodding toward the dog. 'Perra does all the work.'

'Dog?' he asked. 'You call her dog?'

She shrugged. 'It's as good a name as any.'

'How's your sister doing?' he murmured, slapping the dust off his trousers with his low-crowned hat.

'She's better. Battered and bruised, but much better.' Corazón turned toward the house then and cupped her hand up beside her mouth. 'Juanita, Papa, *vienes afuera*. Come outside. There's someone I want you to meet.'

The screen door opened after a moment and the kid sister stepped out on to the shaded porch, bruised up just as Corazón had said, followed by the slender, grey-haired gentleman who could only be the father, and little Miguel.

'Nita,' Carazón began, sweeping her hand toward Jim, 'this is the man who rescued you yesterday. Papa, I'd like you to meet Jim Wolfe.'

The old man came down the steps smiling and thrust out his hand. 'Ah, *señor,*' he said evenly, 'you are my new best friend. Anyone who would stand up against Jack Whelan for the sake of a simple Mexican peasant girl is deserving of great respect.'

'I didn't know who was who,' Jim replied, gripping the father's hard hand. 'I just knew it wasn't right.'

'Still,' the scrappy sheepherder murmured, 'you are a man among men and you are welcome in our home. I am Pedro Alvarado, head of the family.'

'I'm pleased to meet you, sir. Your daughters have a lot of character, and I reckon it must come from you.'

'Come, *señor,*' the old man said, nodding toward

the porch, 'sit in the shade while we finish our preparations. Nita, where are your manners? Get Señor Wolfe a cup of coffee.'

Jim followed the slender father back to the porch with the little border collie close on his heels, and took the chair the old man indicated.

Pedro's gaze drifted over his visitor, then he spoke in a rasping whisper. 'You probably don't remember me from Sonoita; I wore a younger man's clothes then, but I remember you very well. The whole town was grateful for what you did.'

'Again,' Jim muttered, 'I didn't know who was who. I just knew it wasn't right.'

The old man nodded his understanding and sat down in the shade.

'We are fortunate to live in such a great country, *señor*. The Homestead Act, which was passed during your great war, said that any adult citizen, or intended citizen, who had never borne arms against the government, could claim one hundred and sixty acres of land.

'All I had to do was tell them that I intended to become a citizen, promise to build a dwelling and cultivate the land, and, after five years, the land would be mine, free and clear. Where else could a poor Mexican shepherd be given such a boon?'

'And you've been here for five years?' Jim asked quietly.

Pedro bobbed his head and smiled. 'We were among the first. We trailed our flock north through the valley of the Ajo, pushed them up on to the plateau near Black Mountain, and have been here ever since.'

'You've done well for yourself.'

'I like to think so,' the old man murmured. 'But it's for my children that I labor. Many of my countrymen come north of the border with no hope, no ambition, and end up being no better off here than they were under Maximilian.

'Here, at least, our efforts benefit us, not the rich *hacendados*.'

'And that's the way it should be,' Jim replied.

Juanita returned to the shaded porch and handed him a mug of steaming hot coffee.

'I don't believe I thanked you for rescuing me yesterday, Mr Wolfe.'

'No thanks needed, miss,' he said evenly. 'I'm just a little surprised the sheriff didn't stop it.'

'There is no sheriff in Greasewood, Mr Wolfe,' she said in a hoarse whisper. 'Jack Whelan makes the rules and everyone obeys them . . . or else.'

CHAPTER FOUR

Miguel, with a one-hole guitar slung over his back, swung the corral gate open, stepped inside, and called the dog softly. 'Perra, away from me.'

He waited a long moment as the little black-and-white fur ball moved slowly to the back of the pen, then lifted his hand and pointed.

'Walk up.'

Perra approached the rear of the flock with her tail down but without barking and, amazingly, the sheep started flooding out through the gate.

Jim swung into the saddle, heard the creak of wheels coming up beside him, and turned to see Corazón and young Juanita on the seat of a converted farm wagon that looked for all the world like a miniature version of a prairie schooner.

Corazón hauled back on the long reins and pulled a big Missouri mule to a stop beside him.

'I wish herding cattle was that simple,' he said easily, watching the drive begin.

'Is that what you do?'

He shrugged at her question but didn't avert his eyes. 'I've been kicking around out here a long time, miss,' he said, 'and I guess I've done just about everything there is to make an honest dollar: scouted for the Army, punched cattle for a while, even tried my hand at hard-rock mining, and damn me if I still ain't living from hand to mouth.'

She rolled those huge, black eyes of hers at his response and changed the subject. 'Those are odd boots you have on.'

He looked down at his knee-high moccasins and lifted his hands nonchalantly. 'Given to me by a friend. Nedni Apache. You can tell by the turned-up toes. Makes it so you can't wear spurs to jangle in the night or reflect sunlight during the day.'

'I never thought of that.'

'You would if you were chasing Apaches.'

She nodded that she understood, and ducked her chin at the flock.

'Sheep are afraid of anything that might be considered a predator, Mr Wolfe, and that's how they see dogs. An all-black dog will spook the sheep and make them nervous as it moves around, but an all-white dog can't get any respect at all from a flock of sheep.'

She slapped the reins down on the mule's rump and the wagon started rolling forward in the wake of the flock.

'What about those?' he asked, jerking a thumb at the three fawn-colored Spanish mastiffs ambling along beside the wagon.

'They're guard dogs,' Juanita chimed in. 'Most will just warn you when a coyote or a mountain cat is near, but these are big enough to be able to attack.'

He nudged the grulla into a slow walk and rode close beside the wagon. 'Your father's not going?'

'No,' Corazón replied quietly. 'There's enough work to do around the place to keep him busy and he'll fend for himself while we're gone. He'll ride up to the meadow every week or so, bringing supplies to us, maybe spend the night, then come back down. It's like that every year.'

Jim tilted his head at her answer. 'That sounds a little shaky to me.'

'How so?'

'I don't know. This has all the signs of turning into another classic sheep war.'

'Sheep war?'

Jim turned to her, squinting in disbelief and not quite trusting his ears.

'You haven't heard of them?'

She met his eyes and lifted her free hand in uncertainty.

There was, he knew full well, in every stretch of pasture land from Sonora to the rolling hills of Montana, a line beyond which sheep could not go, where sheepherders could not live in peace, and it had always been so.

No fence stood there, no signpost marked the boundary, but it was there – just as plainly as if it had been scratched in the dirt – and cattlemen would fight to the death to maintain it.

There was nothing about it written down in a statute book somewhere, either, but it was a law nonetheless, and everyone knew it.

Problem was, how did he explain it to Corazón Alvarado?

'Oh, lady,' he murmured, 'there've been several of them. All over the West. Colorado, Nevada, Montana. A lot of cowboys and shepherds have been killed, along with thousands of sheep.'

'Oh, my,' she breathed.

He paused for a moment, trying to remember the details he'd heard around the campfires at night.

'A few years back some sheepmen from New Mexico drove their flock on to the range of Charles Goodnight. His cowhands drove something like four hundred sheep into the Canadian River and drowned them.

'Cattlemen up in Wyoming attacked shepherds and drove over ten thousand up into the mountains, where they died, and in another battle, over near North Rock Springs, the cowmen drove better than twelve thousand sheep over a cliff.'

Wide-eyed, Corazón could only wag her head. 'I hadn't heard any of that.'

'Well, it's true whether you've heard it or not. I just don't want something like that to happen here.'

'Do you think it could?'

He cut his eyes across to her and shrugged. 'I

reckon it's possible. Whelan wants the whole valley and your family seems to be standing in his way. And, truth be known, he isn't half the man Charlie Goodnight is.'

She fell silent, gazing away at the long slope ahead of them, the stands of pinyon pine clustered along the ridges, the brilliant blue of the high desert sky. Then she whispered a response over her shoulder: 'I hope it doesn't come to that.'

'You and I both, miss,' he muttered. 'We don't have near enough guns to stand against a bunch of irate cattlemen.'

Jack Whelan accepted a cup of coffee from his Chinese cook, heard the screen door slam shut behind him, and leaned both elbows down on the flaking paint of the porch rail. He peered at his gaunt foreman.

'Word in town is that this Wolf jasper rode out to the Alvarado spread this morning,' Whelan muttered, tugging his hat brim a little lower against the sun. 'And I've got no idea what he's up to.'

Jethro Hightower, holding the reins of his horse, snickered half under his breath. 'Probably tryin' to get into that Corazón Alvarado's knickers. That's what I'd be doin' if I rode out there.'

'Yeah, well, you're not exactly James Wolfe, are you?'

'What's that supposed to mean?'

'It means he's the joker in the deck,' Whelan said.

'An unknown. And I don't trust him for a Mexican minute. I want you to ride out there, stay out of sight, and see what you can see, understand?'

' 'Course I understand.'

'Then get to it. Take Frenchy with you. You can ride back in tonight after they've bedded down and tell me what's what.'

He set the coffee down on the porch railing and watched the pallid cowhand saunter away toward the bunkhouse.

A strange one, Jethro Hightower was.

A brute of a man with the mind of a ten-year-old. He knew nothing but pain, revered nothing but punishment, and went out of his way to dish it up to anyone he thought would take it.

It had to be something ingrained in him from his childhood, Whelan reflected. Some environment so severe and on-going that he had never learned anything else.

Still, Hightower knew which side his bread was buttered. He wouldn't lift a finger to do work if he could get paid for doing nothing. That was a virtue that Jack Whelan had found he could twist into any shape he wanted. A look, a scowl, a harsh word was all it took.

Every nuance of it played a part in his quest to secure the valley. And that was just the way he wanted it.

It was so close, he mused, having the entire valley under his control, having the name of the biggest cattleman on the plateau and the sway to name his own price when selling beef to the railroad.

Wes Burleson's outfit, over on South Fork, just wasn't big enough and old George Stottlemeyer, west of the ridge, couldn't cross his range without his say-so, and Stottlemeyer would never ask.

For George that meant a long trail drive, either north or south of Whelan's range, to get to the railhead and even that could only be done once or twice a year.

Basically that put Stottlemeyer out of contention for the railroad market. The railroad had to feed their tracklayers three times a day every day of the week and old George just wouldn't be able to meet the demand.

He was one of the original settlers on the plateau and considered Whelan an upstart. He didn't like him or any man in his crew and there had never been a civil word passed between them.

The upshot of it all was that Jack was holding the reins, able to call the shots, and that was exactly what he wanted.

Dominance.

Just as pure and simple as that.

Still, it had been a hard row to hoe in getting here.

He'd been mightily irritated when his father decided to settle in Brooklyn when they'd crossed the sea from Ireland, but there'd been precious little he could do about it at the time.

He was just a kid, after all, and had no chance at

all to stand up against his father. The old man had been a stevedore in the old country, a mean and hungry existence, and he took no guff from anyone.

With his strength, he didn't have to.

As a boy Jack had read every penny dreadful he could get his hands on about the American West: Dodge City, Santa Fe, Sacramento, and he wanted, more than anything, to see it.

Brooklyn had proved to be a rough borough, not much different from the streets of Dublin really, except for the gangs of Jewish and Italian kids who held sway over every poor soul who happened to stray into their territory.

But he had hardened in the neighborhood, and he'd learned his lessons well.

He'd discovered there were only two things in life that really motivated people: fear and the hope of reward. By the age of fourteen he knew how to use both of them.

He rewarded the people who served him and held the rest in check through fear.

It was such a basic precept that he'd always been a little amazed that more people didn't understand its power.

He hadn't given a tinker's damn about the abolition of slavery; still, when the alderman had drawn his name out of the hat and informed him he'd been drafted into the Army, he had no choice but to go.

It was the uniform that had attracted him to the Fourteenth Brooklyn – the flashy red pants, the havelocks hanging down in back – and he'd felt important wearing it.

They'd marched away to the cheering of crowds, performing their intricate drills down the avenue, but that had been the extent of their glory.

He'd done his part in all of it: First and Second Bull Run, Antietam, Gettysburg; but somehow, the fighting had drained him.

It had been crazy. Every last bit of it.

Marching through the incessant rain, not knowing the first thing about soldiering, eating food that would make a billy goat puke. It had got to him, soured him, and there was no respectable way out.

He'd stayed with it as long as he could. Doing his part, following the asinine orders of officers who had no idea in the world what they were doing, and pretending to be friends with the other men.

The war had carried them south, into the soggy hills of Virginia, across swollen rivers and muddy fields. Past the nondescript little hamlets, the whitewashed churches, and sour-smelling slave quarters.

It was a far damned cry from the bustling streets of Brooklyn.

A far damned cry from any place where he felt comfortable.

The Wilderness Campaign, they'd called it, but all he remembered was slogging through the mud day after bone-weary day. Thrashing through the dense underbrush where they couldn't see the Rebs hiding and soldiers dropping in death all around him.

It hadn't been cowardice that made him call it off, he knew that only too well. It was the absolute insanity of dying for a cause he just didn't believe in.

He hadn't run, like they'd said, either. He'd simply sat down in the thickest brush he could find and let the fight move away from him.

Those uppity bastards from the provost marshal's detail had jumped him where he sat that very afternoon, clapped him in irons, and dragged him back to the regiment.

After the humiliation they'd heaped on him in camp that day, the branding, the stripping away of his accoutrements, the drumming him out of camp, he could never go home again.

There was just too much shame involved.

He'd been forced to wear a hat full time after that – something he'd never done before the war – and had taken to wearing a headband to hide the mark they'd given him.

Unable to find work or even anyone willing to hear his side of the story, he'd been forced to wander. But, wherever he went, it seemed there was always someone who knew his terrible secret and voiced an opinion on his disgrace.

And, of course, he'd never married.

What self-respecting woman would have him?

Night after night he'd sat alone in a rented room, getting comfortable with the idea of shooting himself just to put an end to it all.

Then, when he'd begun thinking more seriously

about taking his own life, it was anger that helped quiet the despair he felt and kept him from getting a gun.

He'd followed what scant bits of information he could glean from listening to conversations in taverns up and down the east coast and made it a sacred quest to even the score with the people who'd done this to him.

One lousy sonofabitch at a time.

Colonel Johnson, Captain Boudreaux, they'd got theirs right enough. One more lead, on Sergeant Striker, working in a freight office in Santa Fe, had started him West.

He'd robbed a bank in Chillicothe, Ohio, for a grubstake, crossed the Cimarron Strip on a stolen horse, and found that self-righteous little toad right where his information had said.

Shot him between the eyes in the warehouse, he did, and never felt the slightest twinge of guilt.

Now it was the Alvarados he had to deal with.

The Alvarados and this guy Wolfe.

'One way or another,' he said to no one, 'they have to go.'

CHAPTER FIVE

The land tipped up steeply east of the valley, the mesquite and teddy bear cholla of the lower desert gradually giving way to manzanita and thick stands of pinyon pine along the ridges.

The sheep followed a wide shelf that angled up the slope toward the north, nipping at grama grass and wildflowers as they walked, with Miguel ambling along behind, whistling occasionally and pointing out strays for Perra to round up.

The miniature prairie schooner trundled slowly up the hill in the churned-up swath they left, straining and creaking with every hard bounce, with pretty Corazón hauling on the reins.

The air was sweeter here, not so parched and full of dust as it was down below, and it was easy to see why the sheepherders didn't much mind the loneliness of the high meadows.

It was a slower pace on the mountain. Hushed and sublime. A place to ponder the meaning of life or read a book from cover to cover without someone reminding you of chores that had to be done.

Jim rode slowly, staying level with the wagon's seat and the women, surveying the hillside above them with a critical eye and scanning the long valley below that angled gradually away to the northwest.

Ahead of him the guard dogs patrolled the wavering edge of the flock, watching for predators. A red-tailed hawk studied them warily from the stump of a lightning-blasted pine and coveys of quail skittered away into the brush.

'So you're the one they call Lobo down in Sonoita,' Corazón said quietly over the groan of the wheels.

Juanita turned her head sharply at the words, arching an appraising eyebrow at the man who'd rescued her the previous day.

'I've been called a lot of things, miss,' Jim replied. 'Most of them not so nice.'

'Strange,' she said softly. 'That's not at all what I heard. I was told you gunned down the bandit called Cuchillo Loco, that you scattered his gang, and saved the town from their raids.'

'That was a long time ago, and Crazy Knife never saw the day he was a match for a .45 caliber Colt.'

'Still, you are a hero to the people of Sonoita.'

'Never tried to be.'

She lifted her hand in resignation, turned the wagon into a flat space beside a small, still lake and drew up.

'This will do for a few days,' she announced. 'There'll be firewood in the pines and plenty of forage and water for the flock.'

Jim scanned the area and nodded at her choice. The lady knew what she was about.

'You want me to unhitch the mule?' he asked, swinging down from the saddle.

'If you wouldn't mind. Juanita and I will get a fire going and start supper. How does *arroz con pollo* suit you?'

'Rice with chicken? Sure. Haven't had that for a long, long time.'

'It's my mother's recipe,' she purred. 'She passed away right after we came north, but I think you'll like it.'

'I'm looking forward to it.'

He turned away, stripped the saddle and blanket from the grulla, dropped the trace chains from the mule, and staked them both out in a deep patch of sideoats grama at the edge of the lake.

He ambled back to the wagon and eased himself down to sit on the wagon tongue.

'Quiet up here,' he murmured.

Juanita was on her hands and knees, blowing gently into the flame of a small fire. Corazón was spreading the legs of an iron tripod and setting it up over the tiny blaze.

'Yes,' she said. 'Sometimes even boring, but it has to be done. Sheep are one of the few animals in the world who cannot survive on their own.'

'I don't understand,' he ventured.

She lifted her eyes to him and the hint of a smile wobbled her lips. 'Without a shepherd to care for them, sheep would die, Mr Wolfe. They can't defend themselves against predators. If they're hurt, they can't heal themselves. If they fall on to their backs, they can't get up. They can't even find their own food.'

'I didn't know that.'

'And now you do.'

'Kind of strange,' he uttered, sweeping a hand toward the flock. 'All the Mexican sheep I've ever seen have looked sort of feeble. Seems like they all had a curved back, thin legs, and not much wool. These look pretty rugged.'

'That's my father's doing,' she said quietly. 'He bought a few Merino rams several years ago and has been breeding out the bad traits.'

She reached over the tailgate of the wagon, hoisted out two three-legged milking stools, and handed him one.

'Here. This will be more comfortable to sit on.'

She lowered herself to the other stool and he watched in silence as she started washing the rice in a smoke-blackened Dutch oven.

'She's a very good cook, Mr Wolfe,' Juanita said from across the fire.

'Please, just call me Jim. I'm not some big Philadelphia lawyer or anything. Just a bone-tired saddle tramp working my way West.'

'After what you did for me yesterday,' she murmured, 'I'd hardly call you that.'

'Nita,' Corazón interrupted, 'hand me that chicken we butchered before it goes bad, an onion, and some garlic. I want to get this meal cooking while we still have some daylight.'

Jim gazed away at the jagged peaks of the Mogollon country around them and pondered his assessment of himself.

A saddle tramp.

That was just about the size of it.

Growing up in the dense Missouri woodlands as he had, he'd just naturally learned to hunt and trap along the way, and he'd been carrying a gun since he was big enough to hold both ends of a rifle out of the dirt at the same time.

The family had trekked across the mighty Mississippi from the high-up hills of Kentucky, looking for a better life. It was only a short time after they'd found a place they could call their own that his pa had the crazy idea that would change their lives for ever.

It wasn't another tiny subsistence farm that the West needed in those times, he'd said, it was building material for a growing land, and it was growing faster than anyone had reckoned.

It had taken the better part of a month for the steam engine and saw blades to show up. Then, almost before they knew what had hit them, they had the first sawmill west of the Big Muddy and were turning out loads of lumber.

The white pine logs floating down the river from the forests of Wisconsin and Minnesota were a never-ending source of material for the mill and, of course, the stands of cottonwood and poplar along the bluffs were always there.

He'd grown up deep in the woods, swinging a broad axe from sunup to can't see day after live-long day for as long as he could remember, snaking logs out of the woods with a team of big Percheron horses, using a peavey pole made for a man twice his size to heave them up on to the mill's skidway. It was the back-breaking work itself that had given him the heavy shoulders and put the hard muscle on him.

His pa provided the lumber for a great many projects once they got started: siding and rafters, barn beams and railroad ties, and he'd given work to hundreds of men, who were either a little down on their luck or just sitting out the winters before they could move on West.

His mind flicked back to his last day at the mill and he remembered his father's gruff admonition before he rode away: 'You'll find that common sense ain't so common out there, Jim.'

He'd been right. Half the people he'd met since leaving Missouri hadn't had the sense God gave a doughnut.

The other half were just plain stupid.

He'd shaken Pa's hand, kissed his ma goodbye one last time, and headed for the Indian Nations on a lineback dun.

He wasn't overly proud of what he'd become – a saddle tramp by his own words – but it was his life and, by God, he was going to live it his way.

He remembered, too, the bitter memories he'd brought away from the war.

It hadn't all been death and dismemberment as most people thought. A lot of it was anger, resentment at the system that had put them in that situation, and there was nothing any of them could do about it now.

The disappointment he'd felt in his elder brother had been the hardest pill to swallow and he clenched his teeth trying to shake the cobwebs of it from his mind.

Tom had been delivering a wagonload of lumber to a farmer way over in Taney County when the war broke out, while he and his pa had stayed home running the mill.

The minute the South called for men his pa up and enlisted in the Tenth Kentucky because that was where the family was from. He himself had signed with a Missouri cavalry outfit because that was what all his friends were doing.

Then, when Tom came home, he found they were both gone and figured, since they were anti-slavery, that they'd just naturally gone with the north. He went up to Kansas the next day and joined a Yankee infantry regiment.

When the war was over and everyone came home

for good, Tom showed up wearing the tattered uniform of a blue-belly infantryman and there Jim stood, dressed in Rebel grey.

They had started talking about their experiences during the war and found they'd both been in the bloody six-week siege that was Vicksburg.

Tom had narrowed his eyes at him then, and said, 'You mean to tell me you were one of them sonsofbitches over there that was trying to kill me?'

All Jim could do was shrug his shoulders. 'Yeah, I reckon I was.'

There was just nothing more he could have said. In their case, it really had been brother against brother.

And that had been the end of the story as far as Tom was concerned. He went his way, Jim went his, and they never spoke to each other again for the rest of Tom's life.

He was gone now, God rest his soul, but the bitterness he'd carried with him never had been resolved.

Jim forced himself back to the reality of the moment, turning his attention to pretty Corazón Alvarado, slicing garlic and dried red peppers into the Dutch oven.

He felt the warm upslope wind that had set the branches to swaying in the dark stand of pines, and spotted little Miguel perched on an outcropping of rock above the meadow, strumming his one-hole guitar and humming an old Mexican song.

Corazón stirred the pot again, ladled up a healthy portion of the *arroz con pollo* on to a blue enamel plate, and handed it to him across the fire.

'Here you go . . . Jim,' she said softly.

He accepted the plate from her, splashed some hot coffee into his tin cup, and forked the first bite into his mouth, fully aware that she was studying him with those flashing black eyes of hers and waiting for some kind of a reaction.

He opened his mouth to speak, but the words wouldn't come.

He had noted how tentatively she'd uttered his name, the very first time she had used it, and he leveled his gaze at her, wondering if there were any chance at all that she could be seriously interested in a guy like him.

Fat chance of that, he decided. A real fat chance of that.

'Are you not married, Jim?' she asked across the fire.

'Not any more.'

'Why? What happened?'

He hesitated for a moment before he answered, groping for the right words and hoping against hope that he'd found them.

'I got married after the war and settled in west Texas, you know? We had a nickel-dime cattle spread out there and I was usually gone all day, dragging them damned hammerhead strays out of the gullies. One day I rode into the yard and found the house burned to the ground, my wife and son both murdered.'

His breath snagged in his throat, but he added one more word.

'Apaches.'

Corazón twisted round, apparently wanting to see his eyes, wanting to read the thoughts behind them, and he went on.

'They had tied my wife over our old iron stove and lit a fire in it so they could hear her scream. My son they just swung by the legs and crushed his skull against the wall.'

He looked away into the darkness and dust-covered grass as he spoke, trying to hide the glint of the tear running down the side of his nose.

'I know that because I caught one of the warriors who was there,' he mumbled. 'He bragged to me about it . . . just before I cut his throat.'

He took a small sip of coffee and fell silent.

Corazón's eyes narrowed at him from the other side of the fire.

'Cut his throat?' she gasped. 'That's was a little cold-blooded, wasn't it?'

'Maybe in your world,' he muttered. 'Not in mine.'

CHAPTER SIX

His gaze drifted over the Alvarado family for a moment and he leaned back against the wagon wheel, waiting for the obvious question.

He knew it was coming. It always did.

'If you don't mind my asking,' Juanita purred across the guttering fire, 'what were their names?'

'Alice and James,' he said past the harsh lump in his throat. 'Little Jimmy. He would have been ten years old now if he'd lived.'

'I had the impression you were friends with the Apaches,' Corazón ventured.

He took a deep breath, exhaled heavily, and met her eyes.

'I wasn't at the time. Matter of fact, wanting revenge on them was what got me started scouting in the first place. Swore I'd kill every one of them I ever found.'

'What made you change?'

'I don't know.' He groaned, glancing away again.

'It's different for the Apache. They've been forced to eke out a living in the most hostile environment on earth and they're good at it. Most white men wouldn't last a week out there.'

'But why would they kill a little boy?'

He raised his hands in surrender. 'Little boys grow up to become fighting men and, like I said, it's different for the Apache. If the *Indaa*, the white-eyes, want fighting men, we just call them up and we have more than we know what to do with.

'For the Apache a boy child must be born, raised, trained and tested before he can become a fighting man. If they lose a warrior in battle, it might be years before they can replace him.'

'I never thought about it that way.'

'Not many people have,' he rasped.

He couldn't control the bitter tears welling up behind his eyes and he clenched his teeth hard together as the flood of hurtful memories swamped his mind yet again.

His pretty little wife and infant son – his whole life – snatched away in the space of a heartbeat and he hadn't known how to react.

Visions of riding into the yard that horrible day spilled into his mind and he wasn't able to block them out. The dry west Texas hills in the distance, the sickly sweet smell of death and charred timber that had hung in the breathless air, the panic that had gripped his throat.

It all came back to him in a staggering rush of pain

and anger and he forced himself to regain his composure.

Finding the tracks of Mimbreno Apaches around the place that day had pushed him over the edge of reason, of rational thought, and the bottom had simply dropped out of his world.

He remembered collapsing to his knees amid the smoldering remains of the cabin, lifting his tear-streaked face to an unseen god, and the tortured, animal scream that had erupted from his throat.

He shook his head. Somehow, he had to let it go.

He watched little Miguel wander down from the hillside, carrying the one-hole guitar like a rifle over his shoulder, and ease himself to the ground between his sisters.

The little Border Collie lay down close to Jim's feet, her chin nestled between her paws, and rolled her big, sad eyes up at him.

He continued talking – thinking out loud in reality – and wasn't at all sure they could even understand what he'd gone through.

'I cried the rest of the day,' he droned, 'face down in the dirt, even though men are supposed to be stronger than that.'

'That's just a saying,' Juanita piped in.

He nodded his understanding, still looking away. 'It was almost sunset before it occurred to me to bury the bodies, and there was nothing but charred wood to make the crosses with.

'I couldn't even carve their names or the date of

their passing on the damned things. There wasn't enough solid wood.'

'I'm so sorry for you,' Corazón whispered over the flames.

Juanita wiped a tear from her eye and wagged her head. 'You must have been devastated.'

He snorted softly. 'You could call it that, I guess. No one in the county had seen the smoke, you know? No one came to lend a hand. Hell, no one even knew they were dead except me. Me and the sonsofbitches who'd killed them.

'It just wasn't in me to start over,' he murmured. 'To rebuild the cabin and marry again. It wasn't in me to go to the church socials by myself, feeling everyone's pity, knowing the women were all whispering about me behind their fans and the men feeling my pain and not being able to do anything about it. No, I'd had enough.

'Whoever found them hammerhead strays and the unbranded calves in the gullies could have them. They could have the buckboard, the harnesses, the dried corn in the root cellar and whatever else was worth carrying away. For me it was the end of an era.'

Corazón shook her head sadly. 'I can't even imagine what you must have felt.'

'It wasn't easy, I can tell you that.'

He reached down almost absently, scratching the little Border Collie behind the ears, and got a quick tail-wag as a reward.

'I don't know how I ended up in El Paso,' he

rambled on. 'Seemed like the horse I was riding at the time just naturally drifted in that direction and I didn't care one way or the other.

'Don't remember the drunk I went on, either, just waking up in a cluttered alley, bleary-eyed and stinking of frontier whiskey. But it was there the insane hatred of Indians welled up in me. *That* I'm absolutely sure of.

'I spent my last fifty cents on a shave and a bath, then drifted north to the little cavalry post at Doña Ana to become a scout for the Army. Of course, I'd been in the Army before and already knew something of their ways.'

He took another mouthful of the *arroz con pollo*, chewed it slowly, and swallowed before he spoke again.

'I didn't give a good Goddamn about their stuffed-shirt officers, their rules and stupid regulations. All I wanted was a chance for revenge. And I got it.'

'You must have been very bitter,' Corazón said, squinting at him in the gathering darkness.

'More than you'll ever know,' he agreed. 'I chased Victorio on both sides of the border, forced old Cochise back into the Dragoon Mountains time after time, and fought almost constantly with Geronimo after Cochise died on the reservation.'

He lounged back on the three-legged stool, gazing into the distance, still thinking about the past and how he'd become what he was.

'I rode into the post at Doña Ana that same day,

told the top sergeant I wanted to sign on as a scout, and he just pointed at this weathered old guy leaning against the corral rails on the far side of the parade ground.

'See him,' he told me. 'He's Chief of Scouts on this post.'

'Smoke Shattuck, his name was, and he knew more about the desert and the tribes who lived in it than any man I ever met.'

He took another swallow of his coffee and continued:

'That old reprobate had been a scout and hunter for some of the wagon trains that crossed the plains after they discovered gold in the tailrace of Sutter's Mill out there in California – one of the better ones, from all accounts – and I had a great respect for his knowledge.'

'Sounds like quite a guy.'

Jim nodded soberly at her words. 'He was that. It was old Smoke Shattuck who taught me to get by out here. It was he who taught me to read and interpret sign.

'Not just the tracks on the ground, either, you know, but other, not so obvious, sign. The way birds and animals act, a piece of thread snagged on a cholla spine, maybe a handful of mesquite leaves that had fallen before they should have, brushed off by a passing horse or man. The kind of sign the average guy wouldn't even notice.'

'And you're good at it?' Miguel asked quietly.

'I get by,' he croaked. 'There are signs to read in people, too, you know? The sharp intake of a breath. A slight hesitation before speaking. Not being able to meet your eyes.

'Dumb little things that you never think about, but being able to spot them in a man has saved my skin more times than I care to admit, and I have old Smoke Shattuck to thank for it.

'It came to me kind of easy, as if I'd been born to the trade, and it wasn't long before I could follow a trail every bit as well as Smoke himself.'

'What became of him?' Juanita asked softly.

Jim cocked his head and peered at her. 'He hung it up after a while and just works at odd jobs now . . . hunting for the railroad or guiding settlers to likely places along the Gila River. Mostly he brings in venison that he can trade for room and board at the old Maricopa House there in Yuma. The reality of it is he just has nowhere else to go.'

The sheep were bedding down for the night; a few were still on their feet as if they were standing guard, the guard dogs were lying in the tall weeds watching for predators, and it was time for him to call it a night also.

He slid his plate and cup into a bucket of soapy water beside the wagon's wheel and met Corazón's gaze again.

'Juanita was right,' he said softly. 'You are a good cook. That was probably the best *arroz con pollo* I've ever had.'

'I'm glad you liked it,' she answered. 'I'll fry you up some chorizo and eggs in the morning.'

'You don't have to go out of your way for me,' he murmured.

She tilted her head, studying him. 'I think I do. It's the only way I know to repay you for what you did yesterday.'

'I didn't stop that beating yesterday to put anyone in my debt, miss.'

'Still,' she purred, 'we are indebted to you. It was an act none of us will forget.'

There was nothing he could say. He lifted his hands in resignation and pushed himself up from the milking stool.

He gazed off to the West then – California beyond the ragged blue mountains across the valley – and decided he should probably be moving on. He'd got everything he'd come to Greasewood to get: a hot meal and a good night's sleep.

Other than the beautiful Mexican girl sitting on the other side of the fire, there was no reason for him to dally around much longer.

Juanita seemed to be recovering from the slapping around she'd got at the hands of Jack Whelan's man; Corazón Alvarado had her own life to live. And he had his.

The chances of their ever getting together were slim to none; it was not a bet he cared to take.

Saying goodbye would be the hard part.

He glanced across the fire at her again and

wagged his head at the hopelessness of it all.

She was out of his reach any way you looked at it; part of a proud Mexican family, for Christ's sake, and him a down-at-the-heels drifter who'd never known much else.

Of course he wanted to settle down. Who didn't?

But it would not be with Corazón Alvarado.

No, all he could look forward to was the desert, the wind and sun in his face and, beyond the jagged mountains out there, the places where no one would care what he was. Where, in the lonely hours of the morning, watching the embers of a campfire breathe and glow and dim, he could remember.

Or try to forget.

Corazón eased herself down to the blanket she'd spread under the bed of the wagon, leaned against the inside of the wheel spokes, and fixed her gaze on the dark form of Jim Wolfe, fast asleep beneath a stunted palo verde tree a dozen yards away and very close to his horse.

He wasn't what she thought of as a handsome man, she mused. Not in a pretty sense, anyway. Rugged would be closer to it. Dangerous.

'So, what do you think of our Mister Lobo, Nita?' she asked into the darkness.

'I think he likes you.'

She snorted quietly. 'That's not what I meant, silly.'

'Yes, it is,' Juanita answered propping herself up

on her elbows, 'and you know it as well as I do.'

Corazón rolled her eyes in the shadows but didn't pursue the argument. Nita was right, and she did know it. It was exactly what she meant.

'What makes you say that?'

'I don't know,' her kid sister murmured. 'I was watching him when we ate, the way his eyes kept going to you, listening to his story.

'He was pouring his heart out to you, Cora . . . hoping you'd understand him . . . and there can be only one reason for that. He's falling in love.'

Corazón snorted again. 'Now you *are* being silly.'

Juanita pushed herself the rest of the way up and began absently finger-combing her hair. 'I don't think so. I may not be as worldly as you, but I think I can recognize when a man is trying to impress a woman.'

Corazón didn't respond but the implications of Nita's words were running rampant in her mind.

She knew full well there was no future for her here in the Greasewood Valley. Very few men of their race had settled here and there was not a single one of them she'd be interested in. Possibly Ramon Chavez, a slender *vaquero* over on the Burleson ranch, but in reality even he had nothing to offer a woman.

The Anglo men looked down on her simply because the family ran sheep, and there was no getting away from that.

It might be better for her if she could persuade her father to move the flock on to California . . . Los

Angeles, maybe, or San Diego . . . but she knew he would never do that.

No, he owned their little spread free and clear and this was where he'd stay.

'There's something about him that sets my pulse racing,' she whispered into the night. 'It's as though I can sense the recklessness in him, the danger, and some hidden part of me wants to experience it. To be a part of it.'

Now it was Juanita's turn to snort softly. 'It's against everything we've ever been taught, Cora. Against every tradition of our people.'

'I know,' Corazón mumbled. 'Still, I'd forsake all that for nothing more than the knowledge that someone actually needed me. It's crazy, but that's the reality of it.'

Juanita, too, was gazing across the meadow at the dark form of Jim Wolfe and she remained silent for a long moment.

She shifted her eyes to her sister, a darker shadow among the shadows, and asked the question she had to answer.

'So, what are you going to do?'

Corazón wagged her head sadly, fighting the urge to just amble across to Jim's bedroll and lie down beside him.

'I wish I knew,' she purred. 'I wish I knew.'

Jack Whelan washed the last bite of beefsteak down with a glass of Madeira wine, dabbed his mouth on a white linen napkin, and raised his eyes to Jethro Hightower.

'Well?'

His foreman stood hip-shot at the foot of the dining room table, eyeing the leftover potatoes and gravy with a greedy stare, then shrugged slowly.

'They trailed all them maggots they got up into the hills this mornin', pitched camp beside that little lake, and just been loafin' around cookin' and jawin' and such.'

'Who all went?' Whelan droned.

'The two girls, that scrawny kid brother of theirs, and this guy, Wolfe.'

'The old man didn't go?'

'No, sir. He's at the ranch by his self.'

Jack tipped another slug of wine into his sparkling crystal goblet, swirled it around, and sniffed it the way he'd seen the well-to-do people back on the east coast do.

'Good,' he rumbled. 'I'm sick to goddamned death of this monkey puzzle. I want those stinking mutton-punchers out of my hair once and for all.'

Almost angrily he swirled the Madeira around in his goblet, watching the blood-red wine run down the curve of the glass with narrowed eyes.

Yes. It was time to make his play.

The Alvarados had been given plenty of time, plenty of warning. They weren't making any move whatever toward pulling out, and Jack Whelan had had enough.

'I want you to take three men, ride out there at first light, and put that old scarecrow out of his misery.'

Jethro grinned. 'You want me to kill him?'

'Damn, Jethro,' Whelan blurted, 'do I have to draw you pictures? Of course kill him. Kill all of them. The sheep, too. Burn everything in sight. Make it look like a band of renegade Apaches came through. Nobody in this little berg will doubt it for a minute and if they do they won't speak up.'

Hightower shrugged slowly again. 'You're the boss. I'll pick the men right after I get some grub in me.'

The diminutive Chinese cook with his braided black queue draped over his shoulder appeared at the kitchen door almost as if he'd been summoned.

Whelan nodded curtly, signaling him to clear the table, and lifted his eyes again to Jethro Hightower.

'You do that,' he murmured, taking another hefty sip of his Madeira. 'In the cook shack.'

With a smug look working its way across his face, he watched his foreman pad from the room with the downcast spirit of a freshly whipped puppy.

It was exactly what he'd expected from the man and he grinned when he heard the outside door swing shut. It was so like him.

By this time tomorrow, he mused, it would all be over. At long last he'd have the entire valley under his sway and could start looking at running in another herd of beef. It might mean a trail drive from Santa Fe or El Paso, but it could be done.

The only thing that could foul it up was this saddle bum, Wolfe, but he was reasonably sure that Jethro could take him down if push came to shove. He was cat-fast on the draw.

The man had only one major problem. . . .

He was stupid as a goddamned bone.

CHAPTER SEVEN

The hillside was blanketed with bright yellow wildflowers, the morning air was alive with the harsh, high calls of camp robber jays and Jim sat up grinning, remembering from his childhood how those pesky damned birds were always attracted to the sound of human voices in the woods.

It meant a chance for them to steal food from a campsite, and they were not even slightly shy about doing it.

A pale-salmon dawn tinged the sky above the serrated peaks to the east of them; there were all the signs of being another blistering hot day.

He dragged the corner of his blanket up over his shoulders for a moment and let his eyes sweep the meadow around them.

The air was still, the fragrance of pine resin strong in it, but there was also a hint of something else. . . .

Smoke?

He narrowed his eyes, peering at the dark woods

above them, then to the valley below, still in the dim shadow of the hills.

There. Off to the southwest. A thin shroud of grey smoke rose steadily into the clear desert air, blotting out his view of the mountains, blotting out a portion of the sky.

He twisted on his bedroll, spotting pretty Corazón Alvarado quietly brushing her long ebony hair beside the wagon.

'Corazón?' he called softly.

When she turned her gaze to him, he ducked his head toward the pall of smoke.

She leaned slightly forward on her milking stool, shading her eyes with a slender hand, and peered into the distance.

'Smoke?' she asked. 'Do you think it's a grass fire?'

'No,' he said evenly. 'Smoke from a grass fire is usually white. That's wood burning and it's coming from down toward the ranch.'

'*Ay, Dios mío,*' she breathed. 'Do you think. . . ?'

'I think we'd better get down there.'

He pushed himself up from the bedroll, hefted the worn saddle and blanket from where they set in the shade, and paced quickly to the grulla.

It took him only minutes to cinch the saddle down, pull the picket pin, and climb aboard.

He nudged the grulla into a shambling lope back to the wagon, reached down and swung Corazón easily up behind him.

'You two keep your eyes peeled up here,' he told

Juanita and Miguel. 'I've got a bad feeling about this.'

'We'll be back as soon as we can,' Corazón added half under her breath.

'And you hang on tight, lady,' he said over his shoulder, 'I plan to bake this trail.'

He felt her arms curl around his torso, and he heeled the mare into a thundering gallop down the same wide shelf up which they'd herded the sheep yesterday.

A covey of mountain quail scurried off the trail ahead of them and a lank coyote that had been sniffing the churned up ground trotted away between a clump of beavertail cactus and some weathered grey rocks at their approach.

Truth be known, Jim wasn't paying any attention at all to them.

His mind was racing as they rode, considering possibilities and reasons, picturing grim scenarios in his mind.

An accident?

Not likely, seeing how careful old Pedro had seemed to be around their place. Knocking over a lamp or letting a cook stove get away from him just made no sense.

He had appeared to Jim to be a very mild-mannered man, proud of his family and the status he'd brought them to. The Mexicans who could claim their own spread on this side of the border could be counted on the fingers of one hand. And Pedro

Alvarado was among them.

If it wasn't an accident there was only one other thing it could be: an outright attack by cattlemen.

The beginning of another sheep war.

In this neck of the woods, that meant Jack Whelan.

Jim held to the churned-up swath left by the sheep the previous afternoon until he reached the floor of the valley, then cut across the yellowed grassland toward the creek bed and the Alvarado ranch house.

He slowed to a canter half a mile out, then to a sobering walk, staring at the wisps of dark smoke still rising from the house, and knowing in his heart that they were too late.

It was a sad ending for a gentle man. A man who maintained the culture of his race and had always put his family first. A man who had everything to gain and nothing to lose.

Except his life.

The ocotillo corral fences were nothing more than piles of white ash now, being fanned and whisked across the barren yard by the sullen valley breeze. The charred adobe walls of the house still stood but the roof was gone, the stanchion poles jutting up at odd angles above the blackened bricks and studded with blood-red coals, like the fantasy eyes of demons in the dark of night. Everything inside had been destroyed.

Old Pedro Alvarado lay face down in the yard, still wearing a pale-gray nightshirt, smeared with blood, and he'd been shot in the back. The powder burns in the cloth said it had been at close range.

Jim swung his leg over the grulla's neck, dropped off the saddle, and turned to help Corazón down.

The instant her feet touched solid ground she rushed to her father's side, fell to her knees, crossing herself, and turned him over on to her lap.

'*Madre de Dios*!' she shrieked into the hush of the morning. 'Who would do such a thing?'

She lifted her face to an unseen heaven, her voice cracked with sorrow and anger, and screamed a question at the sky.

'*Why*?'

There was no answer.

Only the rustle of leaves in the cottonwoods along the creek, the chuffing of the grulla, and the occasional snap of still-smoldering wood.

Her wailing and keening filled the air, echoing faintly from the far hills, being heard and heeded by the wild things sheltered among the pines. The sound quavered like an Apache flute, mysterious and tortured at the same time, and Jim turned away from it, biting his lower lip to hold back the rage.

He had already picked out the hoofprints coming into the yard from the creek bed – four riders, wasting no time – and, from the look of the prints, the attack had come within the last few hours.

'You know the answer to that without asking.' The words came out in a grating, angry whisper. 'Who else but Whelan?'

He cut his eyes up at what was left of the ranch

house, trying to force himself back to the reality of the moment.

It was not an easy thing to do.

'I doubt if there's enough wood left to make a coffin,' he muttered. 'Probably have to just wrap him in a blanket.'

Corazón shifted her gaze up to him then, but her composure, her poise, had completely vanished.

Her eyes were swollen and red, the tracks of tears were sheeting down her cheeks, her lips trembled, out of control, and she made no effort to hide it.

'I have blankets in the wagon,' she blubbered.

A look of wide-eyed panic washed over her face at her own words and she couldn't control the anxiety.

'Oh, my God!' she shrieked. 'The wagon!'

He frowned. 'What?'

'The wagon! We left Nita and Miguel up there with the wagon! Alone!'

'Oh, Christ!' he groaned. 'I hadn't even thought of that.'

He glanced up toward the high meadows, several miles away now, seeing and hearing nothing, but some well-honed inner sense told him there was no time to waste in getting back up there.

'Let me put your father in the shade,' he said, bending over. 'We'll attend to him later.'

'But. . . .'

'Later,' he said more firmly.

Corazón bobbed her head once, almost mechanically, and her face was blanched with despair.

He scooped old Pedro's body up from her lap and rose to his full height. 'Where do you want me to put him?'

'Over there,' she mumbled. She nodded toward the shearing shed and said it again. 'Over there.'

Effortlessly, he hoisted the ashen form of her father up from her lap, carried him across to the scant shade of the shed, and laid him down close to what remained of the wall.

Pacing back to the already winded mare, he swung up into the saddle and reached a hand down for the girl.

'Let's ride.'

The shave held no pleasure for Jack Whelan, even though he rarely had it done.

The black leather Koken chair was as comfortable as it had ever been and Ed Murdock could wield a straight razor with the best of them, but something was pulling Jack away from the pure enjoyment of it.

He stared morosely through the plate-glass window, eyeing the dusty main street of Greasewood, the red, white, and blue candy-striped barber pole on Ed's front porch and the people passing by, but the fragments of thoughts going through his mind wouldn't allow him to relax.

'Somethin' botherin' you today, Mr Whelan?' Murdock asked at his shoulder.

'No,' Whelan murmured, trying not to move his mouth and risk being cut by Ed's razor. 'Not really.'

'Aw, come on, man,' the barber prodded. 'I can read you like the *Police Gazette.* It's that new saddle bum in town, ain't it?'

'Wolfe?'

His mind flared with instant anger at the very mention of the man, and he didn't know why.

In reality, he knew very little about him, only that he had the reputation of being a fighter. True, the man had taken down three of his hired hands, but that was a piddling matter.

What galled him was the fact that this heavy-shouldered stranger seemed to be siding with the Alvarado family, the one remaining obstacle to his having total control over the Greasewood Valley.

In his own mind it was very simple: if you weren't with Jack Whelan you were against him.

That made big Jim Wolfe his enemy.

'Yeah, that's the one,' Murdock mumbled. 'Sure got some sand, that one.'

He stopped shaving Whelan for a moment, slapped his razor noisily back and forth on the worn leather strop, then leaned into him again.

'I hear tell he mought be sparkin' that older Alvarado girl already.'

'That's his affair.'

'Unh hunh. Unh hunh,' Ed droned. 'You was interested her at one time wasn't you, Mr Whelan?'

Jack snorted. 'For a dalliance, maybe. Nothing serious.'

'A man could damn sure do worse.'

Whelan didn't respond. It was nothing but barroom chatter and held no importance for him.

Murdock had been right about one thing, though: this Wolfe character had some sand.

He'd taken Buck Tiller down in the dusty street, backed Jack himself down at the doctor's office, and had outgunned two of his men already.

This thing was rapidly coming to a head and that suited him just fine.

What Wolfe didn't seem to realize was that life was nothing more than a glorified game of winner-take-all poker and the rules were simple. . . .

A man had to play the cards he was dealt and try to make the best of it.

And Jim Wolfe had been dealt a losing hand.

A lopsided grin worked its way across Whelan's face at the thought and he tried, again, to relax.

The swarm of dark Sonoran vultures swinging in great lazy circles over the high meadow could be seen from several miles away and they didn't speak of it.

They both knew in their hearts what it meant.

He felt Corazón's arms tighten around him, felt the jerking of her body, and the warmth of her tears dampening his shirt.

The really sad part of it was that there wasn't a damned thing he could do to console her.

The high meadow stunk to bejesus of death and wet wool as they approached; it looked like a battlefield the day after a fight.

Jim slowed the grulla to a canter at the edge of the slope, peering at the carnage spread out ahead of them, searching the hillside for any sign of further threat.

He spotted nothing to be alarmed at but rode cautiously, nevertheless.

Coyotes crept away in bunches, tails between their legs, as they rode in, and the vultures wasted no time in descending.

They were awkward birds on the ground, screeching loudly, folding their great wings, hopping clumsily along with a hitch in their stride, wary and watchful lest the carrion happened to move; then, reassured, they stepped up on to the carcasses and began to feed.

It was hideous to watch and, at the same time, difficult to ignore.

Corazón let out a screech of agony when she saw the bodies of Juanita and Miguel lying dead beside the wagon, both shot through the heart, and there was nothing he could do to soften the pain for her.

She slid off the grulla's rump the instant the horse stopped moving, wailing pitifully into the thin mountain air, and rushed to the bodies.

Jim sat the grulla for a long minute, watching her body quake with sobs, searching for something profound he could say to ease the anguish that was swamping her, and he came up empty.

Her entire family had been wiped out in a matter of hours and it was probably the most senseless act of brutality he'd ever seen.

'*Dios mío*!' Corazón howled into the brassy sky. '*Ay, Dios mío*!'

He swung down from the saddle, ground-hitched the mare, and paced slowly to her side.

She turned into him, unashamed, hiding her face against his chest, her body shaking, trembling, and he wrapped his arms around her, trying to give her some sense of safety, of comfort.

It was the only thing he could do.

'You want to bury them here?'

'No,' she blubbered against his chest. 'Back at the ranch. Next to Papa.'

He nodded his understanding, burying his face in her hair, and speaking as softly as he could. 'You got any sewing gear in the wagon?'

'Yes. Why?'

'It'll be better if we stitch them up in blankets before we haul them down the hill.'

'It'll take a little time,' she croaked.

'You take whatever time you need, little girl. That's the one thing we've got plenty of.'

Sheep lay in clumps of threes and fours, dead where they'd been shot, and others, deliberately drowned, clotted the surface of the lake like foam on a tall glass of beer.

Even the dogs had been shot. The three big Spanish mastiffs lay scattered across the hillside where they'd been watching for predators, and the feisty smaller Border Collie, Perra, close beside the mule. All gunned down simply because they were there.

Amazingly, the wagon was still intact and the mule was unconcernedly cropping grama grass a dozen yards away, not even slightly fazed by the death heaped all around her.

The grulla's ears perked forward at that moment and she turned sharply, peering up the cluttered slope.

Jim followed her look out of pure habit and spotted the riders, four of them, sitting their mounts on the steep hillside above them. Even as he watched one of them lifted a saddle rifle to his shoulder and squeezed off a shot.

Jim dove for the trampled weeds of the high meadow, taking Corazón down with him, and glanced quickly around for something that offered better protection.

The shot clanged off a wheel's iron rim close on his right side and whined wickedly as it ricocheted away into the blazing sky.

The sound of it angered him more than the shot itself.

'Lousy sonsofbitches!' he blurted.

'Who is it?' Corazón asked.

'It's got to be Whelan riders. The ones who did all this.'

He sprang to his feet, slid his own saddle rifle out of the boot, holding low over the grulla's back for an uphill shot, and pulled the trigger.

The dry-gulcher on the far right of the group was hurled back over the rump of his horse, his rifle twirling crazily in the air for a moment before it clattered down among the rocks.

The other three dug rowels into their horses' flanks at the shot and charged away to the north.

'Enough of this!' Jim shouted. 'It's time for some payback!'

CHAPTER EIGHT

Clamping his teeth hard together, Jim vaulted into the saddle, jacked another shell into the Winchester's chamber, and heeled the grulla hard in the ribs. The mare buck-jumped into a headlong gallop along the slope even as he lifted the rifle to his shoulder again.

His shot clipped off a branch above the ambushers' heads, but they hit the open slope at a full gallop, a hundred yards ahead of him, and after that he couldn't tell how wide of the mark his shots were.

He cursed silently that none of them was going down and charged on after them, steering the grulla with his knees, feeding new cartridges into the chamber, and squeezing off shots when he thought he had a reasonable chance of hitting someone.

The mare had been ridden hard today; he knew she was badly winded and running out of bottom, but she kept going, on across the yellowed slope, instinctively dodging the outcroppings of rock, the clumps of cholla.

Sunlight was quickly fading from the sky, the shadows of the pines growing longer; mountain quail skittered out of the way as he rode, and still he couldn't pull within pistol range of the bushwhackers.

Too late he spotted them, sitting their horses in the dark shade of a pinyon grove, and he heard the sudden, startling racket of their gunfire.

It was a trap.

Baited with bad blood, sure as hell, and he'd ridden into it like a greenhorn.

He felt the gut-wrenching shock of a bullet tearing through the muscle of his thigh, a pine branch whipped at his face, and, almost in the same instant he felt the grulla stumble and pitch forward into a fall.

He couldn't be sure, of course, but it seemed the same shot that ripped his leg had killed the horse and there was not a damned thing he could do.

Jim caught one last glimpse of the dry-gulchers hazing their horses on to the north as the mare was going down. It made no sense to him.

Any man in his right mind who was out for a kill would stick around and make damned sure the job was done.

These didn't, and that told him something.

He tried to kick free of the saddle, knowing what was to come, but the foot on his suddenly wounded leg didn't want to cooperate. It hung in the stirrup and there was no time for him to react.

He grimaced at what he knew was coming, felt

himself being flung to the side, going down with the horse: he landed flat on his back, with a heavy grunt in a dark clump of rocks.

The rifle clattered sideways into the high grass, the wind gushed from his lungs in a choked squawk, his vision narrowed and went suddenly black.

He lay there for some time, gasping for even the tiniest sip of air in his lungs and thanking everything that was holy that he wasn't dead. Thanking everything that was holy for that tiny bit of reprieve.

Only slowly did his vision return to normal.

His bad leg was pinned under the grulla, his saddle rifle lay in the grass a few feet away; he glanced around warily – as far as he could turn his head – hoping against hope that the bushwhackers who'd chopped him down didn't come in to finish the job.

It would be just like them.

There was no further movement that he could see against the dark pines; he heard only the normal, expected, sounds of the high desert twilight: the quivering of leaves above his head, the tentative call of a cactus wren emerging from her nest, and the ponderous wingbeats of a hunting owl.

He spent several minutes pushing against the saddle with his good leg, trying to pull himself out from under the grulla; it wasn't working.

He wrapped his hard hands around an outcropping of rock just within reach, then, using the strength of his shoulders and arms alone, he eventually managed to drag his leg free of the dead mare.

He lay gasping for air yet again at the effort.

He could hardly see the wound in the gathering darkness under the trees, only enough to know that the bullet had gone clear through and hadn't shattered the bone.

Slowly, methodically, he pulled his worn belt from the loops of his trousers, wound it around his thigh, and cinched it as tightly as he could, to act as a tourniquet.

Gritting his teeth at the pain, he clawed his fingers into the rocky soil and dragged himself across to the spot where his Winchester lay.

With the saddle rifle firmly in his hands again, he let his eyes slide shut and tried to concentrate.

He was in trouble and he knew it.

Wounded and on foot, miles from any kind of assistance; it was a sure bet that Whelan's hired guns were still out there somewhere, hunting him with the persistence of a hungry bear.

It was going to be a long damned night.

He wasn't so sure he could make it out of there on his own, especially with a game leg, and he didn't know if Corazón could find him.

In reality he couldn't even be sure she was still alive. The bushwhackers could have gone back after her just as easy as not.

There was nothing he could do about it either way it went.

Using the rifle as a makeshift crutch he forced himself up from the ground and hobbled back to the dead mare. He knew he had half a box of lucifer matches in his possibles sack and there would be firewood back among the pines.

There was a beat-up coffee pot in the possibles sack, too, a chipped enamel cup, and half a bag of Arbuckle's Best grounds.

With any luck at all, he decided, he might be able to get a fire going and a hot drink in his belly.

It would be a small enough blessing.

Holding his breath, he untied his possibles sack, and worked the blanket-covered canteen out from under the grulla.

Almost as an afterthought he loosened the cinch on the saddle and worked the horse blanket out, too.

It didn't smell too pretty, but by God it would help keep him warm in the chill of the coming night.

He spotted a sort of hollowed-out dish in the ground, on the downhill side of a thick-bodied pinyon with a few exposed rocks scattered around the roots. It was a likely-looking spot for a cook fire, and Jim searched the woods around him one more time.

It was tomb-quiet out there, and he made his decision.

Yes, he would risk a fire.

He scraped together a pile of twigs, thumbstruck one of his precious matches and, in a matter of minutes, had a small fire going.

Heaving a long sigh of relief, he held his hands out to the flames, flexing his fingers and warming his palms in the scant heat they gave off.

He filled the beat-up coffee pot with water from the canteen, dumped in a handful of grounds, and set it on a rock to boil; it was a task he could have done blindfolded, still, he felt better for the doing of it.

He eased himself down to lean back against the piñon, waiting for the coffee to brew, and pondered all that had taken place in the last two days.

He owed Jack Whelan for all of this, and the time for talk was over.

He had a serious score to settle with that deranged sonofabitch and there was nothing for it but to get it done.

If he could just survive the night.

Corazón Alvarado was cried out.

Everything had happened too fast, too close together, and she was drained.

She rolled Juanita's body on to the patchwork quilt their mother had made, folded her hands carefully across her midriff, brushed the long ebony hair away from her face, and sat back gazing morosely at her remains.

'You had a beautiful life ahead of you, baby sister,' she murmured. 'Children and grandchildren gathered at your feet, a wonderful husband who worshipped the ground you walked on and would bring you flowers just because it was a Tuesday.

'You would have had a house overlooking the

ocean, as you always dreamed, with a red-tile roof and hummingbirds drinking from flowers outside the window. You would have been happy there, content, I know it in my heart, and I am so so sorry that someone took it all away from you simply because your family raised sheep.

'If I can, I'll make them pay for this, *mi hermana*, and I'll keep you in my prayers forever.'

She folded the ends of the quilt up over Juanita's feet and face, tugged the long side flaps snugly across her body, and began slowly stitching them together.

It took far longer than she had thought it would and she kept glancing up at the lengthening shadows on the slope.

Finished at last, she spread another of her mother's quilts for little Miguel and eased his frail body up on to it.

'*Pobrecito,*' she said softly. 'Poor thing. You never had a chance at life, never knew the love of a woman or the respect of men. Never had a chance to build toward your own dreams or taste the bittersweet memories of days gone by. And now those things will never be.

'You were always respectful to our father and always did more than your share. You would have been a good man wherever you went in life and it breaks my heart that you are suddenly gone.

'*Vaya con Dios,* little brother,' she whispered. 'Go with God.'

Without another word she folded the quilt up over

the body of her kid brother and set to stitching it up.

She tucked a wayward strand of hair behind her ear when she was done and lifted her gaze to watch the sun drop behind the mountains across the valley.

Strangely, a feeling akin to fear began swamping her mind.

It had been foolish of Jim to go after Whelan's men alone and he should have been back long ago.

She fed another piece of pine into the guttering fire, then stood and pulled her father's old Colt Army revolver from its compartment under the wagon's seat.

He had never carried the gun as a weapon: kept it only to scare away coyotes, but he had taught her to use it and she could generally hit what she aimed at.

She lowered herself to sit on the milking stool again and thumbed open the loading gate to check the pistol's load. It was full and she breathed a sigh of relief.

What had happened to Jim?

Her entire family had been killed in a matter of hours, the sheep were mostly gone, even the dogs; big Jim Wolfe was the only person she knew whom she felt she could rely on.

Truth be known, she didn't have any real friends in this sad little place.

Oh, she talked to Mrs Gunderson at the general store and Rosa at the hotel on occasion; she'd spoken to Hoot Rafferty at the livery when she bought grain for the mule and Doctor Morales when

Papa needed medicine. But they were not people whom she considered real friends. None of them had ever visited the ranch and they had never socialized away from work.

This Jim Wolfe, now, he seemed sincere enough and he'd done more for her in two days than the rest of them had in all the years she'd known them.

He was the closest thing to family she had after what had just taken place.

Still, she wasn't quite sure what to make of him.

He was an intriguing man, for sure. Caring, honest to a fault, and had an ingrained sense of right and wrong. He seemed to be that rare man who could show both strength and tenderness at the same time, yet never be taken for granted.

Still, when it came right down to it, he owed her nothing.

The setting sun worried her. Owls were beginning to call from the pinyons, a sure sign that night was close, and far off she heard the sad yapping of a coyote.

Strange, in a way. There was still a pack of coyotes gorging themselves on the carrion lying around the high meadow, yet a single one was crying in the distance.

She twisted on her seat and scanned the darkness gathering around her, completely lost in her thoughts. What if Jim were out there, injured perhaps, and hoping she'd come for him?

What if he were dead?

Then, too, there was always a chance that the riders who'd fired at them would come back. The only protection she had was Papa's old pistol, and it would be three against one.

She glanced across at the mule, contentedly cropping grass close beside the small lake, and knew what she had to do.

Clear, oyster-white light from the new moon was beginning to flood the high meadow when she climbed up on to the mule.

She had no idea in the world if she'd be able to find Jim among the pines and rocks of the slope, but knew she had to try.

He would have done it for her, she was sure of that, and it was, after all, on her account he was even out there.

She still couldn't decide what to make of him.

She'd been involved with only one man in her entire life: handsome Felipe Figueroa, son of Don Hernan Figueroa, the biggest landowner in the Sonoita Basin, and she pondered that brief interlude as she rode.

They had developed a friendship in the pastureland across the river, which had escalated into an intimacy all too soon, and she had been under the impression that they would be married.

Then, when she broached the subject to Felipe, he had laughed in her face and told her in no uncertain terms that she was beneath him, a diversion only, and moved on.

Her heart had withered and died within her at the rejection but there had been absolutely nothing she could do.

Now, as she became interested in this Jim Wolfe, she felt her desires stirring again.

Dark clumps of teddy-bear cholla shone like silent black sentinels in the graveyard stillness of the slope, and she gave the mule her head, letting her pick her own way northward.

What could she possibly say to Jim to make him understand the anguish she'd been dealt the last time she'd become involved with a man? What could she say to explain the risk she'd be taking by putting that behind and opening herself up to him?

Opening herself up to the possibility of another horrible heartbreak. Another kick in the teeth.

Maybe it would be best to just lay her cards on the table. Face up. Just tell him how she felt and let the chips fall where they may.

Maybe she should just shut up about it. Let the whole thing go. Let him get on with his life, whatever that was, and pretend none of these feelings she had was real.

She could go on being the spinster Mexican girl everyone took her for and life would go on as it was.

Then again, what kind of life would that be? Hiding the pangs of jealousy she felt every time she saw one of her friends and their broad-shouldered husbands together. Wishing some of that happiness – even a little bit of it – could be hers.

Even as she thought it, she knew she could never do it.

No, she had to take the chance. One more time.

It scared her.

The moon was already bright when Jethro Hightower and the others clattered across the wooden bridge and into the yard of the Whelan ranch house.

Jack stood stolidly in the light of a lantern on the porch, having been alerted to their arrival by the hollow thudding of the horses' hoofs coming across the bridge.

'I thought there were four of you,' he challenged.

'There were,' Hightower mumbled. 'McMurty come down with a sudden case of lead poisonin'.'

'Wolfe?'

' 'Course it was Wolfe. You reckon any of us would've gunned him down?'

Whelan snorted at the question. 'Sometimes I wonder.'

He took a step forward, out of the lantern light, so he could see Hightower's eyes a little clearer. 'You get them all?'

'Got the old man first thing this mornin',' Jethro said with a satisfied grin working its way across his face. 'Took out the younger girl and that scrawny kid brother of theirs before noon.'

'What about Wolfe and the girl?'

Hightower shrugged his sloped shoulders. 'Girl's still up there in the hills, cry-babyin' it like there's no tomorrow, and for her there may not be.'

'What about Wolfe?'

'Plugged his ass good and proper, I did.'

Jehtro chortled out loud, a wheezing, choking laugh, wiped his eye on the back of his fist, and went on:

'He come chargin' across that slope like he thought he was the Ninth Iowa Cav and I lifted his ass clean outta the saddle. One of the best shots I ever made.'

'Was he dead?' Whelan demanded.

Hightower shifted uncomfortably on his feet, his eyes darting around as if he were searching for a plausible answer and couldn't find one.

Unable to stall much longer, he glanced worriedly back up at Jack Whelan.

'Had to be, boss,' he mumbled. 'Him and his horse both went down and he didn't move any more. Leastwise I didn't see him move any more. Maybe a twitch or somethin' like that, but no real movin' around.'

'But you didn't check?'

Jethro hung his head then, again unable to meet Whelan's eyes.

'Wasn't no need to. I know damned well I burned him.'

'But you didn't check,' Whelan said again.

He turned away, wagging his head at the foreman's stupidity, and paced to the door, which stood open behind him.

What he wouldn't give for a crew of men he could depend on.

'I swear, Jethro,' he said over his shoulder, 'if you had a brain you'd be dangerous.'

CHAPTER NINE

His name was being called over and over again.

'Jim? . . . Jim? . . . Jim?'

A soft voice, almost tender.

'Jim?'

Then, for some reason, the voice became angry, belligerent, and he didn't know why.

'Jim! . . . Jim!'

The voice started shaking him, jerking him hard, and he didn't like it.

'Jim!'

At first he had thought it was just part of the odd dream he was having, but little by little it became more real, more sensible, and he knew he had a fight on his hands.

He doubled his fist down by his thigh, where the voice wouldn't see it, and cracked his eyes open just the tiniest, merest squint.

All he needed was a target, the chin maybe, just a point of reference, and he'd knock this sonofabitch out with one punch.

It was Corazón Alvarado, kneeling close beside him, gently shaking his shoulder and he frowned, not quite understanding all this.

The shaking stopped and the ebony-haired angel smiled at him. 'Thank God! I got so worried when I couldn't wake you. Are you all right?'

He wagged his head uncertainly, trying to clear the tangle of cobwebs from his mind; and his throat was parched.

'I've been better.'

'You got hit in the leg,' she murmured.

'Yes.'

'Do you want me to look at it?'

'Where am I?'

'In the high meadow.'

He let his eyes drift away from hers for a moment, peering into the darkness of the trees around them.

He heard nothing, saw nothing, and he wanted to sleep.

'Do you want me to look at it?' she asked again.

'I don't know what you can do to it out here,' he answered.

He sat up slowly, still searching the darkness around them and trying to make some sense of all this. The only movement anywhere close was from the big Missouri mule, stamping her hoof impatiently a few yards away.

'How'd you find me?'

'The smoke,' she whispered. 'I smelled the smoke.' She fed a broken pine branch into the tiny fire, but didn't look away.

'Lucky I had a match,' he muttered.

'We should get you back to the wagon so I can take a look at this,' she said, nodding toward his leg. 'I have a needle and some silk thread in case you need stitches.'

'Got any whiskey?'

She smiled at him, warm and slow and understanding. 'Half a bottle of Bacanora mezcal. That's what Papa always drank when he was up here.'

'That'll work.'

He pushed himself up, using the saddle rifle as a crutch again, and stood scanning what he could see of the high meadow in the clear, cold moonlight, listening for anything out of the ordinary: the chink of a bit, the creak of leather, stone clicking against stone.

It was an old habit.

There was nothing out there and he forced himself to relax.

'How about if you drag that lop-eared hay burner over,' he said quietly, 'and we'll see about making tracks out of here.'

He waited until she had led the mule back to the fire, then he grabbed a handful of mane and heaved himself up on to its back. It took a moment of wriggling to sit up and straddle the animal, sparing his bad leg as best he could, then he reached down and swung Corazón up behind him.

'Which way?'

'South,' she answered, pointing a finger back

along the slope. 'Just keep the hill on your left and we'll find it.'

He tugged the mule's head round to the direction Corazón was pointing in, nudged the mule into a slow walk, and settled in to the unfamiliar gait of the animal.

His mind was still a little muddled from the disjointed dream he'd been having, certainly it was not clear enough to guide the mule through the clumps of cholla showing in the wan light of the moon. He gave the animal her head and let her pick her own way south.

'You get the bodies stitched up in blankets?' he croaked over his shoulder.

'I did,' Corazón answered, 'but I'll need help getting them on the wagon.'

'We'll manage,' he said quietly. 'We don't have much choice.'

Corazón wrapped her arms around Jim's waist, lay her cheek against the corded muscles of his back, and let her eyes slide shut.

He smelled of perspiration and pine needles, of wood smoke and old leather, and she just didn't care.

He was here. He was alive. He was someone to cling to.

And she desperately needed someone to cling to.

Everything she knew was gone. Everything familiar. For the first time in her life, she felt completely vulnerable.

They moved slowly through the darkness with the small husking sounds of the night all around them, the pale moonlight making lacy patterns through the leaves, letting the mule pick her own way between the stands of pinyon pine and clumps of cholla that studded the high meadows.

After the better part of an hour they reined in at the wagon. She slid down, added a few pieces of kindling to the sputtering fire beside the wagon, and turned to help ease Jim off the mule on to his good leg.

'Sit here,' she said, motioning toward one of the milking stools, and steadied him by the arm as he did so.

'You mentioned something about mezcal?' He wiped a hand across the stubble of his beard and she picked out a strange worry in his eyes.

'I'll get it,' she answered. 'I'll have to slit your pants leg to look at the wound, Jim, but I can sew it back up when we're finished.'

'Right now I'm more concerned with getting a drink in me.'

'Men!' she uttered. 'You're all alike.'

But she turned to the wagon, rooted about in a carved drawer for a few seconds, and came out with the bottle.

'Papa always said it was for medicinal purposes only, but we all knew better.'

He pulled the cork on the fat bottle of distilled agave juice, lifted it to his lips, and took the first deep swallow.

'Ahhh,' he breathed after a long moment. 'Your father was a wise man.'

Corazón smoothed her skirt behind her, lowered herself to the other stool, rummaged through a box of sewing material, and dragged out a small pair of scissors.

'Are you ready for this?' she whispered.

'Reckon I'm as ready as I'll ever be.'

Carefully she inserted the tip of the scissors into one of the bloody holes in his trousers, snipped a long opening over the wound, and spread the material open.

'The bleeding has stopped,' she murmured, 'and it looks as though the bullet just ripped a big gash in your leg. That means it will take a lot more stitches to close it.'

He cocked his head. 'Do what you have to do, miss. The way I kick around out here I can't afford to lose a leg.'

She dug around in the sewing box for another brief moment, then held a curved suture needle up in the weak light of the flames for examination.

'That's what you're going to use?' he asked quietly.

'I've used it before,' she said. 'When one of the sheep got cut. It works a lot better than a straight one.'

'I'll take your word for it.'

She bobbed her head at his answer and squinted, threading the needle by the flickering light of the fire, then she lifted her gaze back to him.

'This is going to hurt.'

'It won't be the first time I've been hurt,' he mumbled.

He took another swallow of the fiery mezcal and handed the bottle back to her. 'Spill some of this on it. Might numb it up a little.'

She did as she was told, squeezing the wound together as best she could, and heard his sharp intake of breath when she started the stitches.

'I'll be as gentle as I can,' she purred.

He snorted softly. 'I knew that without you having to say so.'

She met his eyes for a fleeting second then, a hopeful question suddenly quirking her mind.

What did that mean?

'You must be hungry,' she said without looking away. 'I don't think you ate at all yesterday.'

'Didn't have time,' he replied. 'You didn't get to eat, either.'

She nodded, her hand rolling neat stitches through the gash in Jim's leg. 'I wasn't hungry.'

He fell silent then, watching as she tugged the slack out of the silk thread and tied the final knot in her handiwork.

'Nice job,' he said quietly. 'I was afraid I'd have to cauterize it.'

'I'm glad you approve, sir,' she murmured. 'Would you like me to cook you something?'

'I could eat,' he mumbled with a nod. 'I want to get some sleep, too. I've got a feeling tomorrow's going to be a long, long day.'

Corazón didn't respond right away, cleaning the curved needle and putting everything back in her sewing box first, then lifted her eyes to his.

'You can lie down under the wagon if you want to, Jim,' she said softly. 'I'll wake you when it's ready.'

He didn't argue the point and she was glad for it. There had already been enough unpleasantness for one day.

The vultures returned with the first rays of morning sun, screeching at each other and ruffling their huge wings, trying to establish some kind of pecking order among themselves. The coyotes, of course, had never quit.

The stench hanging over the high meadow on this second day of death was almost unbearable.

Corazón held a perfumed bandanna over her nose as she turned the chorizos in the skillet, and Jim had to content himself with inhaling the aroma of the Arbuckle's coffee in his cup.

She glanced up from her cooking and caught him staring at her from the wagon tongue. 'How's your leg?'

He shrugged. 'Feels better. I reckon I can walk on it now. Probably be limping for a while, but I think I can walk on it.'

'Good,' she droned. 'I want to get out of here.'

'I'm with you on that,' he said, jerking his head toward the meadow. 'If I never smell this stink again, it'll be too soon.'

Corazón wagged her head dubiously. 'Do you think you can load Juanita and Miguel on to the wagon?'

'Should be able to,' he said, pushing himself up. 'They can't neither one of them weigh a buck twenty.'

She lowered her eyes, picked the chorizos out of the black iron skillet, cracked eggs on the rim, and spilled them into the hot oil. 'This will be done in a few minutes.'

Jim hobbled to the rear of the wagon, picked up the bodies stitched into clean patchwork quilts, and laid them gently on the tailgate. He rigged the tie-down ropes over the unfamiliar load so they wouldn't fall out on the ride down to the ranch and paced slowly back to the fire.

Corazón handed him a plate of chorizos and eggs and waved him toward the milking stool. 'I don't know when we'll get to eat again,' she said, 'and I wish it were something better.'

'Don't worry about it, little lady. I'm guessing you've got other things on your mind.'

'Yes,' she said glancing away. 'We'll have to bury them before we can do anything else and there's no priest anywhere near to give them absolution.'

Jim didn't respond. There was nothing he could say.

Every bit of this bloodbath could be laid squarely on the doorstep of Jack Whelan, he thought grimly. The murdered family, the sheep, the dogs, the burned out ranch . . . all of it.

The man was loco.

Well, he'd called the tune, he'd had his goddamned dance, and now it was time to pay the piper.

They ate in silence with no pretense of etiquette. They ate because they were hungry, because they were running out of time; when they were finished Corazón slid the dishes into a bucket with a half-hearted promise to clean them up later.

Jim backed the mule into the trace chains, rigged the collar around her neck, adjusted the long reins, and hoisted himself up to the wide bench seat as Corazón stowed the cooking equipment inside the wagon.

With everything in place she climbed up to the seat, using the spokes of the wheel as a ladder.

She smoothed her skirts behind her, dropped down on the seat beside him, and picked up the long reins.

'I'm not so sure you can handle the brake if we need it,' she said with a disheartened sigh.

He shrugged, leaned back against the puckered opening of the wagon's stained cover, and watched as she slapped the reins down on the mule's rump.

The churned-up slope was becoming familiar to him after all the comings and goings they'd been doing on it, and he grimaced at the thought.

'This isn't over, you know that, don't you?' he asked quietly, bracing his good leg against the footrest.

'Yes,' she said with a nod. 'Whelan has gone too far.'

'There's not a court in the land that would convict him of any wrongdoing in this. He's made the whole thing look like an Indian attack.'

'I know,' she agreed. 'But there haven't been any hostile Indians around here in years.'

Jim shook his head. 'No, this is going to come down to a simple case of gun law and he's got the most guns.'

'It doesn't matter one way or the other,' she said. 'Either I'm going to kill him or he's going to kill me. I have nothing left to lose.'

'I wouldn't go so far as to say that.'

'It's true, anyway,' she murmured. 'The family is gone, the ranch is gone, even the flock is gone.'

She lifted her eyes to him then and continued. 'The only thing I have left in the world that means anything at all to me is you, Jim. And I don't know how you feel about that.'

He let his gaze sweep the coarse grasses of the slope for a moment, searching for the right words, then he turned to her again.

'When I saw you holding your sister up in the street the other day,' he said evenly, 'something happened to me inside, and I don't know how to explain it.'

'You can try.'

He took a deep breath and exhaled heavily. 'I'm not much, Corazón, and I know it. Nothing to write home about, that's for sure, and I've done some things in my life I'm not so proud of.

'The one thing I always wanted, though, was a place to come home to, a place to hang my hat when the day was done. Having someone around that gave a damn if I lived or died. And I was hoping it might be you.'

He looked away then, unable to meet her eyes.

'I reckon I fell in love with you that very first day,' he murmured. 'I wanted to ask you to be my wife, only I didn't have a damned thing to offer.'

'Some women don't need as much as others, Jim,' she said softly. 'To some women, a good man is enough.'

He squinted at her. 'Are . . . are you such a woman?'

'I am,' she replied. 'And I think you're a good man.'

'Then. . . ?'

She stopped his question with an upraised hand. 'We can figure it all out if we're still alive when this is over.'

He opened his mouth to speak, and again she stopped him with her hand.

'If we're still alive.'

CHAPTER TEN

The pervasive odor of lanolin was gone from the Alvarado ranch when they pulled into it again and it was strangely silent. No more bleating of sheep, no barking of dogs or the clucking of chickens. Only the soft husking sound of a morning breeze stirring through the dry grasses of the field.

They rolled into the yard slowly, rounding up between the hulk of the smoke-blackened house and the shearing shed, then coming to a stop beside a heap of whitish ocotillo ash.

'Not much left of it, is there?' Corazón sighed over her shoulder.

'No,' Jim agreed quietly. 'Not much at all.'

'It reminds me of the plaza in Sonoita the morning after a fandango,' she added, 'only there was no happiness here last night.'

He didn't respond. There was just nothing to be said.

Gripping the edge of the wagon's hard seat, Jim

eased himself down, testing his wounded leg, and offered his hand to help Corazón down.

He unhitched the mule then, tethered her at the water trough beside the burned-out house – the only thing that was still intact – and met Corazón's sad gaze.

'If you've got a shovel around the place,' he said quietly, 'I'll get started on the graves.'

'There should be one leaning against the shed,' she said. 'On the far side, if it wasn't burned up.'

'And where do you want them buried?'

She ducked her head toward a small rise some twenty yards from the house. 'Under that scrub oak tree,' she said. 'We used to sit there in the evenings and I think they would have liked that.'

'Good enough. I'll get started. Are you all right?'

'Yes. I just don't think it's really soaked in yet.'

'What do you mean?' he asked.

She shook her head forlornly and lowered her eyes. 'I don't know. I keep thinking of stupid things like what they would all want for supper, yet I know none of them will be here to eat.'

And again there was nothing he could say.

He started away toward the shearing-shed, glancing back at her after every few steps, found the shovel right where she'd said it would be, and paced on toward the scrub oak.

The death of a family member was never an easy thing to face, he reflected, and Corazón had a lot on her plate.

Her entire family had been taken from her and they had been her whole life. The bond she'd had with them, the blood connection, couldn't be denied, and there was nothing he could do about it.

He slammed the blade of the shovel into the leaf mold and loam under the tree, digging the graves side by side, and not all that deep.

He'd grown up swinging a broad axe in the dense Missouri woods. It had filled out his shoulders as a young man, put the heavily corded muscles in his arms, and work came easily to him.

Still, it was hot work, even with the weak valley wind that stirred the leaves above his head, and he paused several times to mop his brow and wipe the sweatband of his low-crowned hat.

Corazón had wandered away toward the meandering bed of Kitchen Creek when he caught sight of her again, apparently gathering her thoughts and a few wildflowers for her family's hasty graves.

His heart went out to her, knowing it could not be an easy thing to do.

He remained quiet while she was gone, lowering the bodies into the graves, piling the dirt back in, and covering them with heavy adobe bricks from the charred ranch house to discourage coyotes and the big Sonoran vultures from digging them up.

He waited under the oak for some length of time before she had dried her eyes and returned carrying thick bunches of purple thistle to put on the graves.

From somewhere she produced a black and silver

rosary and lowered herself to her knees beside the shallow graves.

'*En el nombre del Padre,*' she began in a subdued voice and Jim fell silent out of respect for her faith.

He watched as she ran the black beads through her fingers, gradually working her way around the necklace, praying fervently between the sobs that quaked her body, and heard all too clearly the sorrow that ebbed and flowed in her words.

When she was finished, she crossed herself several times and wiped her eyes on the back of her wrist one last time.

There was no priest for miles around to say the last rites for her family and there was just nothing else for it.

She placed her simple offering of thistle blossoms on the three graves and rubbed the side of her finger where one of the spines had stabbed her.

'Rest in peace,' she said finally. She rose to her feet then and turned to the heavy-shouldered drifter she cared so much about.

'Are you ready for a war?'

'Too bad I had to leave my saddle up there in the hills,' Jim said. 'That represents a month's wages for a cowhand, and we could have used it right about now.'

'We'll manage,' she answered.

He didn't respond, just hoisted himself up on the mule's back and offered her a hand to climb up behind him.

He nudged the mule forward, walking past the little knoll south of the house, both of them gazing morosely at the new graves there, and remaining silent out of respect.

'Is there any kind of short cut to the Whelan spread?' he asked. 'I've got a bad feeling about taking the road.'

Corazón looked up. 'Do you think he'd be watching the road?'

'Hard to say. He might not know we're on our way.'

She ducked her head toward the cottonwoods along Kitchen Creek. 'We can cut through the woods there. It'll be slower going but, if he's watching the road, it might be safer.'

'That's what I'm thinking, too.'

He heeled the big mule into a trot, pulling her head round toward the cottonwood and willow thicket that lined the creek.

'How many men you reckon he's got working for him?' he asked over his shoulder.

Corazón hesitated a moment before answering. 'There are probably nine or ten more,' she said close to his ear. 'And not a single one of them would think twice about killing us.'

'Ain't that always the way of it?'

After several minutes he edged the mule into the dappled shade of the trees, hearing the soft gurgling of Kitchen Creek beyond them and the high-pitched calls of cactus wrens and jays.

The valley sweltered in the late-summer heat and there was not a cloud in the sky. The mountains seemed to lift and waver around them, the smell of bursage was strong in the air, and sound seemed somehow muted beneath the trees.

They rode slowly, wary and watchful for any sign of danger, avoiding possible ambush sites. Jim carried the Winchester easily, cradled in the crook of his elbow.

Again he gave the mule her head, letting her pick her own way through the maze of trees, jumping ahead in his mind, trying to picture the possible scenarios they might run into at the Whelan ranch.

That there would be gunplay when they rode in was almost a foregone conclusion, the severity of it depending on how many of Whelan's gunhands were on the place.

And he had to be ready for anything they threw at him.

The most likely scenario he could picture was that they'd be challenged in the yard. One or two men, in all probability, with possibly one or two more covering them from windows and doors.

If that came to pass, it would be root hog or die.

And he wasn't quite ready to die.

After an hour of steady riding Jim eased into the shade of a scraggily cottonwood tree on a slight rise to give the big mule a breather, braced his hard hands against her withers, and squinted at the summer-yellowed valley ahead.

Still a ways off, he could make out the buildings of the Whelan ranch: white-painted frame structures with weathered roof shingles curling in the relentless high desert sun. He narrowed his eyes to study the place.

'You ever been in there?' he asked the girl.

'A few times,' she replied quietly. 'That low building on the left is the bunkhouse. If there's anyone still at the ranch, that's where they'll be.'

'Anything special I should know before we go traipsing in there?'

She shrugged. 'They're on the far side of the creek and there's not really any good place to ford. He's got a wooden bridge built over the creek that makes a sort of hollow echoing sound whenever someone rides across it and they know you're coming quite a while before you get there.'

'Perfect,' Jim muttered. 'That means we won't be able to catch them flatfooted.'

'No,' she agreed. 'They're holding a pat hand.'

'Yeah, and it's going to be a bag of nails when we get there.'

'What does that mean?'

'Confusing,' he answered. 'Things happening way too fast. You think you're ready for it?'

'As ready as I'll ever be,' she said, and her voice was thick with bitterness.

He nudged the mule on ahead, emerging from the fringe of trees on to a wide stretch of pastureland. The field before them was dotted with dusty clumps of prickly pear cactus and ocotillo showing darkly against the summer-dried grasses. Jim was fully aware that they could be seen from the ranch house.

The muscles at the corners of his jaws bunched into hard knots as he steeled himself for what lay ahead. He heeled the mule into a canter across the wide field, heading for the foot of the bridge.

Corazón had been right. The mule's hoofbeats produced a loud, booming sound as they rode across it.

Fifty yards ahead of them he spotted a slack-jawed man come out of the bunkhouse, step down into the yard, and stand straddle-legged waiting for them to arrive.

It was almost exactly the scenario Jim had considered. One man challenging them in the yard, but he saw no gun barrels protruding from the door or windows and no movement behind them.

Jim reined in ten yards short of the man and felt Corazón slide off the mule's rump. He swung his leg over the mule's neck and dropped down on to his good leg.

'Who are ya and what d'ya want?' the man rumbled.

'Jack Whelan around?' Jim asked flatly.

'Who's askin'?'

'Name's Jim Wolfe.'

The cowhand squinted at him with dull eyes and cocked his head. 'I'm Jethro Hightower,' he mumbled. 'Foreman.'

'I've heard of you, halfwit,' Jim replied. 'Heard you like to shoot people in the back.'

'Yeah?' the foreman asked. 'Well, I ain't goin' to shoot *you* in the back, hoss.'

Hightower's eyes narrowed, his fingers twitched near the butt of his six-gun.

He was getting ready to open the ball.

Jim knew it was coming.

They both went for their guns at the same time but, before either of them could clear leather, another pistol shattered the noonday stillness close beside him.

Hightower reeled backwards a few feet, a gaping hole between his eyes, and spilled on to his back. His legs quaked once in the dry dirt of the yard, then he lay still.

Jim jerked his head to the side and saw Corazón glaring at the man's body, the smoking Colt Army still in her slender fist.

'Damn, lady,' he muttered, 'you're almighty fast on the draw.'

'It's not what you think,' she said. 'It was already out.'

They heard the thundering beat of horse's hoofs galloping away from behind the bunkhouse, and they looked up in time to see a rider bent low over his horse's withers, and racing away toward town.

Jim swung the Peacemaker up and squeezed off three quick shots. They were all clear misses and he lowered the weapon again, choosing instead to save the ammunition.

'Well,' he muttered, 'it's a lead pipe cinch that Whelan will know we're on our way now.'

'You think there's any more of them in there?' Corazón asked, nodding toward the bunkhouse.

'I reckon we'd better check. The big house, too. No point cashing in our chips this early in the game.'

Together they paced toward the low, frame bunkhouse, both of their pistols raised and at the ready, but there was no sign of life to be seen.

Cautiously they stepped inside, scanning the shadowed corners, smelling the stale odor of cigar smoke and unwashed bodies.

Rumpled bunk beds lined both walls, a long table sat in the middle of the room, replete with dirty coffee mugs, a tattered copy of the *Police Gazette*, and a dog-eared deck of playing cards spilled sideways.

A pot-belly stove stood prominently at the far end of the room with cluttered counters on both side of the stovepipe. A peeled tree branch nailed up in the corner with black rain slickers dangling from it was the nearest thing to a closet in the entire space.

'What a pigsty,' Corazón uttered. 'Someone actually lives in this mess?'

'The whole crew apparently. Reckon they've all gone to town with the bossman,' Jim said after a moment.

'Good thing,' she agreed. 'He's going to need all the help he can get.'

Jim snorted softly at her words. 'I'll drink to that.'

She glanced toward the open door, sudden doubt spreading across her face. 'Do you think they might be forted up in the big house?'

He shrugged. 'Only one way to find out.'

CHAPTER ELEVEN

They went out of the door together, scanning the wide yard and the windows of the ranch house for signs of danger.

Nothing out of the ordinary caught their attention, so after a minute they stepped down to the hard-packed earth of the yard and marched on across, alert and apprehensive.

The house was well built and massive. A railed veranda ran all the way across the front of the place, tall plate-glass windows stood like sentinels in the shadow of the porch roof, and leafy green vines trailed down from planters on the second-floor balcony.

They climbed the steps to the porch slowly, Jim with the heavy Peacemaker aimed squarely at the door and Corazón with her old Colt Army tastefully hidden behind the folds of her skirt.

Without a word Jim stretched a hand out for the doorknob.

He heard the sharp intake of startled breath at that moment and a slender Chinese coolie threw the door wide open, bowing repeatedly and deeply from the waist.

He wore the traditional long jacket and loose trousers of the Chinese peasant, clean and crisply pressed, and a long, black queue draped over his shoulder, smelling faintly like oysters fresh from the sea.

Jim narrowed his eyes, the Peacemaker weaving slowly back and forth across the Celestial's midsection.

'Who are you?'

'I cook,' the man answered in a shaky croak. 'Name Ah Chan. I go now.'

'Hold on a minute,' Jim ordered. 'Is there anyone else in the house?'

'Only housekeeper, Tong Chiu.'

'And where would he be?'

The cook tilted his head and frowned slightly at Jim's question. 'Tong Chiu female.'

'All right then,' Jim said with an exaggerated grimace, 'where is *she*?'

'She in kitchen.'

Almost magically a tiny Chinese woman, also wearing the long jacket and loose trousers of a coolie, appeared behind him. Her clothes were a pale grey whereas Ah Chan was wearing blue.

She, too, bowed from the waist several times but didn't presume to speak.

'I go now,' the cook repeated. 'Tong Chiu go, too.' He turned on his heel without waiting for permission and paced quickly out of the room.

Jim eased into the huge room when he was gone, wary and on edge, glancing left and right for hint of a trap and aware that Corazón was right behind him.

'Will you look at this guy?' he asked quietly, sweeping his hand at their surroundings. 'Persian carpets on the floor. White linen tablecloth. Crystal goblets. Madeira wine. The sonofabitch was living like a king on other people's misery.'

'That was his way,' Corazón ventured bitterly. 'Trying to be something he never could be.'

He nodded his agreement and exhaled heavily.

'You look around down here, Corazón,' he mumbled. 'I'll check upstairs.'

He moved away from her, eyeing the second floor landing, then taking the stairs cautiously. He heard no footfalls above him but still he trod lightly with the heavy Colt held at chest level and ready to use.

A long hallway with several closed doors along it opened to his right off the landing. He paced along it as quietly as he could, easing each door open as he passed and giving each room a cursory look, but the house appeared to be empty.

He heard the front door open and close downstairs and moved quickly to the window of the room he was in to see if possibly some of Whelan's men had returned unexpectedly.

Instead of hired gunmen, he spotted the two

bandy-legged Celestials plodding steadily away toward the wooden bridge over the creek. They each wore a wide, conical straw hat and carried a small carpetbag. There was very little difference in their heights and the only way he could tell which was which was by the color of their clothes.

'Don't blame you a bit, folks,' he said to no one. 'This job just didn't have much of a future.'

He turned his back on the departing pair and continued on to the next room.

There was no sign of life on the second floor of the ranch house and he concluded that Ah Chan had been telling the truth when he'd said the housekeeper was the only other person there.

Corazón waited for him at the foot of the stairs with arms folded across her chest; she shook her head when Jim started down.

'The place is empty,' she said evenly.

He lifted his hands in resignation and stopped close beside her. 'You want to burn the place down like they did yours?'

She shook her head. 'No. This was Jonah Bennett's spread and I'm pretty sure he'll want it back once Whelan is out of the picture.'

'Why did Whelan choose this place to settle?'

'Why not? It's far and away the best house in the valley, the closest to town, and it has good water.'

He nodded at her reasoning. It made sense.

Even to a drifter.

*

Jack Whelan splashed another shot of raw frontier whiskey into his glass, tossed it down, and let his eyes roam the dark interior of the saloon.

His men stood in clumps of twos and threes at the bar, others lounged around the battered card tables, and he was glad they were there.

It was coming, this showdown with Wolfe.

After the mess Jethro had made of it up in the hills, it couldn't be any other way.

He knew full well it took a certain type of man to stand up against the kind of odds he had working for him – a full dozen gun hands on the payroll and the total complacency of the town.

He knew, too, that Jim Wolfe was that type of man.

What the hell was that sudden tightness he felt in his belly?

Fear? Anxiety?

No, it was something else, but he couldn't put a name to it.

His eyes scanned the room again over the shot glass and he nodded his approval almost imperceptibly.

Hard men they were. They did what they were told without question, rode for the brand, and weren't opposed to shedding a little blood when the time came.

Many of them had been with him from the beginning and he knew their little quirks and weaknesses: this one a drunk, that one a womanizer.

It was a necessary evil for a man who ruled by power.

He heard the heavy thudding of a horse's hoofs at

that moment and glanced out of the window in time to see Travis Cooper haunch-slide his mount to a stop at the hitching rail.

Cooper was a native-born Texan, knew his way around cattle, which was something Whelan himself did not, and he would fight at the drop of a hat.

He piled off the strawberry roan he rode, took the steps two at a time, and shouldered his way through the saloon's rickety batwing doors.

'They're a-coming, Mr Whelan,' he called across the room. 'They're a-coming.'

Jack held up his hand to silence the man and motioned him over to his table.

'I'd appreciate it if you'd hold it down a little, Travis,' he said calmly. 'No need for the whole crew to know my business. What happened?'

'Well, sir,' Cooper sputtered, 'that there Wolfe jasper and little Corazón Alvarado rode into the ranch – on a mule, they was – and Jethro met 'em in the front yard. They had words, pulled iron, and Jethro went and got himself killed.'

'Wolfe outdrew him?'

'No, sir, it was that Corazón bitch took him down and I seen her do it.'

'Corazón?' Whelan blurted. 'Well, I'll be damned. I didn't think she had it in her. You think they're on their way here?'

'Why, I'd practical guarantee it.'

Jack tented his fingers above the scratched table-top and leveled his eyes at the rangy cowhand. 'All right then; if Jethro's out of the picture you're going to be my new foreman.'

'You mean it, sure enough?'

'Yes, I do. And, for your first job as foreman, I want you to round up the men and stake them out as snipers. A couple of riflemen on top of the buildings, some covering the doors and windows, and it's fifty dollars in gold to the man who takes this sonofabitch down.

'You might as well stop by the bar while you're at it and get yourself a couple shots of bottled courage.'

'Don't need to worry your head about me, Mr Whelan. I got enough by God courage for the both of us.'

Instant anger gripped Whelan at his words and he hissed a response through clenched teeth.

'Just get on with it.'

The new straw boss gave him a disparaging smirk, turned on his heel, and sauntered away toward the bar.

'Gather round, boys,' Cooper called. 'We got us some work to do.'

Whelan narrowed his eyes at the man's back, wondering – yet again – if any of his men knew about that goddamned brand he'd been blessed with at Spotsylvania Court House.

Somehow that question was never very far from his mind.

He let his gaze slide to the streaked window again and pondered what Cooper had told him.

This Jim Wolfe was badly outgunned to be coming here and he had to know it. His only real chance would be in mounting some kind of surprise attack. The back door, maybe, or through an open window. Something that would not expose him to the hail of gunfire he'd walk into if he tried to come in through the front door.

He cut his eyes across to the back wall of the saloon, trying to remember what was in back of the place. A pile of litter, he remembered that, then nothing but a sloped expanse of high desert. Yes, there were a few trees back there, palo verde and scrub oak, a few waist high bushes, but nothing that would hide a man.

Wolfe would have to be almighty damned canny to make it this far without being seen and, realistically, Jack didn't think he could do it.

He wasn't some wild-ass Apache, after all, and he was not a small man by any stretch of the imagination.

No. He'd be seen.

And he'd be shot.

Whelan grinned at the thought. The Alvarados out of his hair. Jim Wolfe out of his hair.

His goal of becoming the biggest cattle baron on the Mogollon Plateau was clearly in sight now.

And it couldn't come too soon.

'Cooper,' he called across to the bar. 'I want the front *and* the back covered.'

Travis nodded his understanding. 'You got it, boss.

You got it.'

Whelan hoisted the whiskey bottle and emptied it into his glass.

Yes, he did have it. He *always* had it.

He wouldn't tolerate anything else.

CHAPTER TWELVE

Jim heaved himself up on to the powerful mule's back, hoisted Corazón up behind him, and nudged the animal into a canter toward the bridge.

'I think we'd better stay off the road,' he rumbled over his shoulder. 'I've got a bad feeling about that.'

'Do you still think they're watching it?' she asked close to his ear.

He cocked his head. 'Wouldn't you be if you knew a man bent on killing you was headed your way?'

'Yes,' she sighed, 'I guess I would.'

'Our best bet will be to shelter ourselves from sight in the trees along the creek again and pray Whelan doesn't have patrols of men out gunning for us.'

They clopped noisily across the wooden bridge over the creek and he scanned the area ahead of them with a wary eye.

Everything was coming to a head with the Whelan outfit. He knew that without even have to think about it.

A few more hours, that would be about it. He'd

either be pushing up daisies or on his way to California with a new bride at his side.

It was all in the hands of God now and he knew that, too.

'You know the trees give out before you reach town, don't you?' Corazón murmured. 'Right where the creek comes down out of the hills.'

'Yeah,' he answered, 'I remember that from when I rode out here the other day, but there's precious little we can do about it.'

He tugged the mule's head round toward the cottonwoods in spite of her warning.

There really wasn't much choice.

'Does Whelan have someplace special he goes to when he's in town?' he asked, nudging the mule into a slightly faster gait.

'The saloon is the only place I'm aware of,' she replied as they eased into the mottled shade of the trees. 'I've heard he has a private room on the second floor.'

Jim nodded that he understood. 'He'll be holed up there then, and probably backed by a dozen guns. Is there a back way in?'

He felt her wag her head behind him and knew the answer before she spoke. 'No. The only obstruction to their view will be the buildings themselves.'

Again he nodded. 'Well, we can't ride down the main street bold as brass, can we? They'd pick us off before we got within a hundred yards of Jack Whelan.'

He squeezed his eyes shut for a moment then, trying to recall the lie of the land around Greasewood.

The slope on the east side of town had slightly more brush on it if he remembered right, mesquite and ocotillo, and a few outcroppings of rock that he'd seen when riding in.

That would definitely be the way to go.

They could take what cover they could get from the brush and ride in slow to avoid raising a dust. Still, he felt pretty sure that, if Whelan had lookouts or riflemen posted on the rooftops, they'd be spotted long before they got close enough to do any damage.

It was quiet under the trees. The only sound was the whisking of the mule's hoofs through the bed of dead leaves and the gurgle of Kitchen Creek some twenty yards away. Small birds flicked from branch to branch around them and a mule deer with a hefty rack of antlers soared over a bush off to the right and disappeared down the slope.

After an hour's ride the trees thinned out. They forded the creek where the rutted wagon road crossed it, edged into the fringe of cottonwood and willow on the south side, and worked their way up the slope a couple hundred yards before emerging from the trees again.

The settlement of Greasewood was clearly visible a mile or so to the south but there was no sign of any imminent danger; no throngs of townsfolk heading for the hills to get out of harm's way or freight wagons being set up across the street as barricades.

The only movement he saw was the dark curves of a pair of Sonoran vultures riding the air currents high above their heads.

He reined in at the edge of the trees, rubbed a hard hand across the stubble of his beard, and studied the slope east of town.

'We'll swing wide up the slope,' he said, ducking his head toward the hill, 'and try to come in behind the livery stable.'

'Whatever you think is best,' she murmured. 'Just get me within pistol range.'

Jim bobbed his head ponderously and nudged the mule forward again.

Get me within pistol range?

That might be easier said than done.

He angled up the slope, pausing often behind the taller brush and outcroppings of rock to look, to listen, to feel.

There was still no sign of activity in the settlement below them and he forced himself to breathe normally.

It was much slower going than he would have liked, but it felt safer to take his time about riding in and, in spite of the urgency he felt, he decided to follow his instinct.

The sun was well past its zenith, glaring down on them from a cloudless, brassy sky, when he finally turned down the slope toward town.

This would be the tricky part and he knew it all too well.

There would be less cover and they'd be much more visible as they got closer to the settlement.

Any lookout worth his salt would pick out the furtive movement coming down the slope toward town, as it was always movement that attracted the eye in the wild.

He narrowed his eyes and mumbled a prayer half under his breath. A little luck, that's all they needed.

Just a little luck.

CHAPTER THIRTEEN

'The men are all in position, Mr Whelan,' Travis Cooper said across the marred table.

Whelan looked up from his empty shot glass and arched an appraising eyebrow at the lanky Texan. 'That's good to know, Trav. How have you got them arranged?'

'Well sir, they's two on the roof, one covering the front and one covering the back, they's two watching the back door, two more watching the front, I got three more at the far end of the bar, and I'll be up at this end covering you.'

'Tell me something in all seriousness, Travis. Did you run out of breath saying all that at one time?'

Cooper recoiled slightly at the question, blinking in sudden surprise, then got his wits about him. 'Well, a-course I did. Who wouldn't?'

Whelan wagged his head dubiously, squinting at the man. 'That's all the men we've got left?' he asked.

'Yes, sir. Counting me, we got ten men.'

Jack didn't respond. He cut his eyes over to the back door and the far end of the bar, assuring himself that it was as Cooper had told him.

Without a word he turned and checked for the two men the new foreman said he'd posted at the front door. Satisfied, he poured himself one more shot of frontier whiskey, tossed it down in a single gulp, and pushed himself up out of the chair.

'You just make damned sure they're all alert and ready, understand? I'll be upstairs for a few minutes getting myself ready.'

'You can count on me, Mr Whelan. You can damn sure count on me.'

'For your sake,' Jack rumbled, 'I hope so.'

The entire place lapsed into silence as he ambled toward the stairs, and he was fully aware that every eye in the room was fixed on his back when he started up.

Strangely enough, it didn't bother him. He was used to being gawked at and, truth be known, he rather enjoyed it.

He turned into the narrow second floor hallway at the top of the stairs, paced to the last door on the left, and stepped inside.

He remembered in vivid detail the day the establishment's owner had bounced an aging whore out of the room and told him to consider it his own.

'I will,' he'd said. 'And let no one else enter it.'

The room still smelled of cheap perfume and sex, even after having been cleaned several times, but that didn't bother him, either.

In reality, that was the least of his worries.

It was an unpretentious room; a bed still stood in the corner, a chest of drawers with a wash basin and pitcher of tepid water on top a few feet away, a table and two chairs were planted squarely in front of the small, streaked window, and he had a change of clothes in the wardrobe behind the door.

A framed photograph of a Southern plantation house hung from one of the papered walls but, other than that, there had been no attempt at decoration.

He closed the door behind him, fished a long steel box from the chest of drawers, set it on the table in front of the window and took a seat.

He had a reason for coming to the room, he thought as he opened the box.

A very critical reason.

And he didn't have a lot of time.

'You two get in here,' Rafferty barked from the barn door. 'I'll hide the mule in one of the stalls.'

He stepped aside waiting for them to ride in, his forehead furrowed in frown, and asked the question that had been plaguing him all day.

'What the hell happened?'

'Whelan,' Jim said simply. He threw his leg over the mule's neck, slid down, then turned and lifted Corazón off. 'They killed old Pedro Alvarado at the ranch. Burned them out. Then, when me and Corazón went down to check, they hit the sheep camp in the meadow. Killed Juanita and little Miguel, all the dogs, and ran most of the sheep into the lake.'

'Damn!' the hostler blurted. He turned to Corazón and shook his head. 'Sorry to hear about your father, miss. I always had great respect for him.'

'Thank you,' she said softly. 'I'm still trying to understand it.'

The liveryman glanced back up at Jim and his words came out like a judge's verdict.

'Whelan's stepped way too far over the line this time.'

'You're telling me,' Jim agreed. 'Way too far for it to be ignored.'

'They get your mare, too?'

'Yeah, and that was a damned good horse. How's the coffee holding out, Hoot?'

Rafferty pointed toward the stable's tiny kitchen with his chin and started away with the mule. 'Pot's on the stove, just like always. Even dropped a couple of eggshells in there to settle the grounds this time. You two help yourselves, I'll be right back.'

Jim paced into the shadowed kitchen without waiting, clunked the Winchester down on the rough-sawn table, and splashed hot black coffee into two dented cups that he picked off the shelf.

'The whole town knows there's a fight coming,' the hostler uttered when he stepped into the kitchen. He pulled an old clay pipe from his pocket, tamped down some rich Virginia tobacco, and lit it with one of the new-fangled lucifer matches he'd struck on the seat of his trousers.

'I wouldn't doubt that,' Jim answered. 'It's overdue.'

'Just the two of you?'

Jim nodded somberly. 'Yeah, but she's pretty handy with that old hog leg of hers.'

'Well, I'm on your side,' Hoot stated. 'You know that. I got me an old Spencer that ain't seen any action for a couple of years now.'

'Anyone else?'

The hostler cocked his head and shrugged slightly. 'Old man Bennett might drag iron. Especially if he knows he ain't alone. He stands to get his spread back if Jack Whelan is out of the picture. And Morales might pitch in. Hard to tell about him, though. Them doctors is almighty funny about killing people.

'Even at that,' he added, 'them're some short odds.'

'Well,' Jim said, 'it has to come sooner or later.'

He leveled his eyes at the liveryman over the rim of his cup and asked the obvious question.

'Whelan in town?'

'Holed up at the saloon. I seen 'em ride in this morning and I imagine he's got a snootful of pop-skull whiskey in him by now.'

'Surprised he ain't hiding out in the brush again like you said he did at Spotsylvania.'

Rafferty chuckled at his words. 'That makes two of us. They'll be coming for you as soon as they hear you're in town, you know that, don't you?'

'I won't be waiting around for them, Hoot. I plan on taking the fight to them.'

'That'll put a knot in their tails,' Hoot droned. He turned to Corazón and tilted his head. 'You're awful quiet, young lady.'

Corazón just shrugged. 'I didn't come here to talk.'

'My kind of woman,' Jim muttered.

'What does that mean?' she asked, tucking a strand of ebony hair behind her ear.

'It means that, when this is all over, I'll be asking you to marry me.'

'You mean if we're still alive?'

'Yeah,' he replied, 'reckon I do.'

Her eyes widened slightly and she smiled at him. 'And the answer will be "yes" . . . if we're still alive.'

Now it was his turn to smile. 'You got a Bible-thumper in town, Hoot?'

'Got a Justice of the Peace.'

'That'll do.'

He set what remained of his coffee down on the rough-sawn tabletop and pushed himself erect.

'Well, then, let's go see what fate has in store for us. You both ready?'

Hoot bobbed his head ponderously and turned away. 'Will be as soon as I fetch my Spencer.'

Jim hoisted the saddle rifle off the table, levered the breech open to check his load, and they paced out of the barn three abreast with Corazón in the middle.

Without a word between them they stopped in the brassy sunlight and scanned the tiny settlement.

The street was empty, as Jim had expected, but he could see furtive movement on top of the buildings down the street.

'Two on top of the saloon,' he muttered. He ducked his head in that direction and Hoot followed his eyes.

'Snipers,' Rafferty offered. 'Another one on top of the general store.'

'They'll see us coming for a Texas mile once we step out, and I'm thinking we'll have to take them out first,' Jim said in a rasping whisper.

The hostler just shrugged. 'Well then, let's get 'er done, Johnny Reb.'

Jim twisted slightly, sizing up the wiry Irishman. 'You reckon you can hit any of them from here?'

'That one on the store, for sure. He ain't no farther than the last mule deer I took down.'

'Good enough,' Jim replied. 'You take him and I'll go for the ones on the saloon. Those jokers are just begging for it. As soon as we take these guys out, start running for the saloon, take what cover you can find and shoot anything that moves.

'Most of these boys will be ex-soldiers and know how to handle a gun,' Hoot cautioned.

'Yeah,' Jim agreed with a nod, 'but they might not be so willing to die for Jack Whelan. Once they see some of their friends going down, I suspect a few of them may quit.'

He turned to Corazón then, worried for her safety and grateful she was there at the same time.

'Corazón, you run for the doctor's office as soon as we start shooting and fire at anyone showing themselves in the door or the windows. And don't show them any more mercy than they did your family.'

'I hadn't intended to,' she replied quietly. 'It's like you shouted up in the high meadow: "It's time for some payback!" '

Jim lifted the Winchester to his shoulder, aimed carefully for the long offhand shot, squeezed the trigger, and saw the sniper above the saloon jerk backwards.

Out of the corner of his eye he saw Rafferty's man go down also, then a flash of streaming black hair snapped through his field of vision as Corazón sprinted away toward the doctor's office as she'd been told.

He swung the saddle rifle slightly to the right and fired at the other sniper. It was a clear miss.

Another shot sounded up the street at almost the same instant and he saw a rifle barrel being pulled back through a window.

When he glanced up again the third sniper was gone.

'I'm guessing that would be old man Bennett,' Rafferty muttered.

'Well, I'm damned glad he bought in.'

'See you in hell, Jim.'

The hostler scampered away, running in a crouch,

and Jim started, too, in a stumbling run, his wounded leg screaming at the pain, heading for the shelter of the watering trough outside the saloon.

He saw the scrappy liveryman disappear down a narrow alley between two buildings, heard the snap and whine of bullets whizzing past his head, and dove headlong for the scant shelter of the trough.

A barrage of gunfire erupted from Doctor Morales' office across the street behind him, both pistol and rifle fire, and he heaved a sigh of relief for the covering fire.

Stealing a quick glance over the water trough, he spotted the body of a man in a white shirt sprawled across the saloon's doorway, blood staining his shirt-front and his legs twitching in his death throes.

Another man peeked around the edge of a blown-out window at the same time, but jerked his head back quickly as more shots from the doctor's office splattered glass in his face.

After a moment Jim laid the saddle rifle down in the dust of the street, dragged the heavy Peacemaker from its holster, and pushed himself up.

He took the steps up to the shaded boardwalk two at a time.

A hail of bullets splintered the batwing doors of the saloon as he ran, but he was coming on too fast to stop.

He felt the incredible burn of a slug rip through him at the waist; he dove through the bullet-blasted doors, landing on his shoulder, and rolled up firing.

Two men in front of the bar crumpled under his fire and, oddly, the shooting stopped. The bitter smell of gunpowder hung heavily on the air.

A fan of sunlight flooded the room as Hoot Rafferty and a grey-bearded man who, he assumed, must be Bennett pushed in through a back door, their rifles swinging in wary arcs back and forth across the interior.

His eyes settled on Bennett for a split second, sizing him up: a man whose gray hair didn't seem to make him old, whose stooped shoulders didn't take away an impression of strength, and he liked what he saw.

His eyes settled on another man, Jack Whelan, standing behind a table at the far end of the room, and peering at him through those hooded eyes of his.

Another fan of bright sunlight behind him lit the shadowed interior of the saloon at that moment and he was aware that both Corazón and Doctor Morales had stepped in.

Jim rose to his full height from the filthy barroom floor, aimed the Peacemaker squarely at Whelan's chest, and took a few staggering steps in his direction.

'You wouldn't shoot an unarmed man, would you?' Whelan asked into the hush that had settled over the place.

He stood with a tenuous smile touching his lips and spread his arms in an overblown show of innocence.

'Look at me,' he crooned. 'I'm unarmed.'

'Really?' Jim asked flatly, for he'd noted the odd angle – obviously made by the corner of a board – jutting out at the elbow of Whelan's sleeve.

The first time he'd ever seen a sleeve-gun rig had been on a riverboat gambler plying his trade out of New Orleans; he'd never forgotten that single, telltale sign.

He was seeing it again now.

'And what do you call all the hardware you've got up your sleeve?' he rumbled into the hush of the room.

Whelan's smile got even more improbable at his question and Jim saw the sudden, exaggerated stiffening of his arm, saw the tiny Remington derringer leap into Jack's hand from the deep folds of his sleeve, and he fired.

Whelan's shot went harmlessly into the puncheon floor of the saloon.

Jim's slug took the two-bit toff in front of him squarely in the heart.

A wide-eyed look of shock and surprise hit Whelan's pallid face, the backs of his knees bumped the heavy oak chair behind him, and he sat down hard. His head lolled drunkenly forward on to his chest: he was dead.

Jim heard the roar of another pistol shot behind him at that instant, spun on his heel and dropped to one knee, the Peacemaker still at the ready.

He watched as yet another lanky cowhand wilted

to the rough-sawn floor in front of the bar, saw the gunsmoke still leaking from Corazón's big Colt Army, and pushed himself up again.

'That's enough, boys,' he shouted into the room. 'There's no one left to pay you now.'

He stepped round behind Whelan's body, snatched the faded blue headband off the dead man and jerked his head up by a fistful of hair.

'Any of you guys ever see this?' he called, pointing to the burn scar on Jack Whelan's forehead with the barrel of his six-shooter.

'A coward?' a man blurted from behind the bar. 'I'll be damned if I knew that.'

'You in the war?' Jim asked loudly.

'I was,' the man answered. 'Second Illinois.'

'Then you know what this means, and that right there is the brand you boys have been riding for.'

'Well, that does it for me,' the cowhand said evenly. 'I'm a sonofabitch if I'll ride for a coward.'

Jim waited a few seconds, letting the man's statement soak into the other Whelan riders who were still alive and just then were peeking out from behind the bar and the tables they'd tipped over.

'Best bet you boys have is to ride back out to the ranch and see if you can find enough money around the place to make your wages. Then, if I were you, I'd be for trailing on out of here.'

'No more shooting?' the lanky cowhand behind the bar asked warily.

'No more shooting.'

'I'll take you at your word,' the man muttered and rose to his full height. He craned his neck toward the back of the saloon, exhaled heavily, and started for the door.

'Any of you guys with me?'

Four more of Whelan's men pushed themselves up from their hiding-places, slid well-oiled pistols into their holsters, and paced out behind their riding partner.

'See you around, Mr Wolfe,' the cowhand mumbled from the shattered batwings of the door.

'Don't count on it, cowboy. I'll be trailing out of here, too.'

CHAPTER FOURTEEN

They waited until the room had cleared: Jim and Corazón, Hoot Rafferty, the aging Doctor Morales, and old man Bennett, guns still ready for war.

'You OK, Hoot?' he asked the feisty hostler.

'Reckon I am. I didn't get in on much of the fighting, though.' He swept his hand toward the other man and stepped a little to the side.

'This here's Jonah Bennett, Jim. He's the one took out that other sniper.'

Jim slid the Peacemaker back into its holster and thrust his hand out toward the aging man.

'Appreciate your help, Mr Bennett.'

'Didn't do it for you, son,' Bennett said, gripping his hand. 'Did it to get my spread back. I saw a chance and I took it.'

'Still,' Jim murmured, 'I reckon you saved my bacon.'

'Glad it worked out that way, but that don't make us bed partners.'

Doctor Morales stepped forward, nodding at the blood spreading on Jim's shirt and spoke worriedly. 'You'd better let me have a look at that.'

'It's just a scratch, Doc,' Jim said easily. 'At least that's what it feels like.'

'Still, I'd better have a look at it. If we can step across to my office, it shouldn't take too long.'

'Mind the man, Jim,' Corazón murmured. She slid the big Colt Army into the waistband of her skirt and swept her hand toward the door.

'Are you always this bossy?' he asked, but he followed her out.

The sun on the street seemed abnormally hot after the shade of Greasewood's only saloon and the air was dry.

Shopkeepers and their wives stood in small groups along the boardwalk, shading their eyes and waiting for some kind of news about the shoot-out.

Only gradually did the realization come to them that they were no longer under the oppressive thumb of a ruthless Jack Whelan, that they no longer had to cower inside their homes and live in constant fear of his riders.

Jim followed Doctor Morales up the few steps to the covered boardwalk and stepped into the coolness of his office. He dragged a cane-backed chair across the room and sat down, heaving a great sigh of relief that the gunfight was over.

'There's a bottle of *aguardiente* in the cabinet there,' the doctor said softly, nodding at his medicine shelves. 'Just in case any of you need to paint your tonsils.'

'I could use a shot,' Jim said. 'That was a close thing over there.'

'I'll get it,' Corazón murmured, starting toward the shelves.

'You know me,' Hoot chimed in. 'I'll drink to damned near anything.'

'Jonah?'

'Sure, why the hell not?' the grizzled rancher nodded.

'I'll join you when I'm finished here,' Morales added.

'How about you, Corazón?' Jim asked. 'You sure as hell earned it.'

She tilted her head and smiled. 'Just this once.'

'Stand right here, Mr Wolfe,' the doctor said softly, 'and pull your shirt up for me.'

Jim glanced over his shoulder into Corazón's bright black eyes and grinned. 'I know, I know,' he droned. 'Mind the man.'

She just smiled knowingly at him and started tipping shots of the fiery *aguardiente* into the glasses.

Jim tugged his shirt out of his trousers as he'd been told and waited for the doctor to check him over.

'You're right,' Morales said after a minute, 'It's just a flesh wound. It'll leave a scar but there shouldn't be any permanent damage.

'Corazón,' he added, 'if you'll hand me a roll of that gauze and a sterile pad on the counter there, I'll get him bandaged up and you two can be on your way.'

He wiped away the blood still oozing from the bullet burn with another wet towel, set the bandage in place, and quickly wrapped the long gauze ribbon around Jim's waist to hold it in place.

'That should do it,' he announced, leaning back in the chair. 'And now I'll have that drink, young lady.'

'What do I owe you, Doc?' Jim asked quietly.

'Nothing. It's a small enough service after all you've done for the town.'

Jim nodded soberly. 'All right, then. At least you have my thanks.'

He leveled his eyes at the scrappy little hostler. 'You got any good horses we can pick up to ride out of here on, Hoot?'

'Sure do,' the liveryman said. 'A strawberry roan and a lineback dun. They're a couple of Whelan's men's horses and you can have 'em free for nothing. I doubt if them jokers will be needing them any more.'

'Ride out of here?' Corazón asked evenly. 'What about the graves?'

He shrugged. 'I reckon it'll be best if we leave the past behind us, little girl. There's just too many hurtful memories around here. I thought maybe we'd head West.'

'I'm willing,' she answered.

She turned her gaze to the wiry hostler and cocked her head. 'If we're riding out, I want you to have the ranch, Hoot. You'll have to do some rebuilding, of course, but I want you to have it.'

'Aw, don't talk daft, missy,' Rafferty muttered over the rim of his glass. 'There's no way in the world I can afford that.'

Corazón just smiled. 'I didn't say I wanted you to buy it. I said I want you to have it. There's going to be a lot of Whelan stock roaming around out there with no one laying claim to them, and I doubt if anyone in town would fault you for picking up a few head.'

'Wouldn't bother me none if you rounded up some strays and mavericks,' old Jonah Bennett chimed in. 'I'll probably be doing some of that my damned self. God knows Whelan got my stock dog cheap.'

'Most of the walls are still standing, Hoot,' Jim said quietly, 'but the roof's gone and the inside was gutted by the fire. About the only thing left in one piece is the watering trough.'

'And it has a good well,' Corazón added.

Hoot cocked his head, staring at pretty Corazón. 'Are you serious about this?' he asked incredulously.

'Dead serious,' she said with an emphatic nod. 'You put your life on the line for us when few people stepped forward. All I ask is that you maintain the graves of my family on that little knoll south the house.'

'Hell, Hoot,' Jim ventured. 'You could turn Whelan's own branding-iron upside down and make that big 'W' brand of his into a double diamond without even half trying. You don't want to run a livery stable for ever, do you?'

'And we'll probably be coming back through here sometime in the future,' Corazón chimed in. 'It would be nice to know we had a friend here and a place to stay.'

Hoot closed one eye and squinted at her through the other. 'Oh, you'd always have a friend and a place to stay. Nothing to worry about on that score.'

He glanced away into a dark corner of the saloon, a faraway look creeping into his eyes.

'The Double Diamond ranch,' he sighed with a silly schoolboy grin working its way across his weathered face. 'Well, I'll be damned. How can I refuse an offer like that?'

'You can't,' Jim said flatly.

'The graves?' Corazón asked.

Hoot bobbed his head, still grinning. 'Of course I'll take care of the graves. Be happy to. I'll carve markers for them and even plant some flowers out there so the place looks nice all the time.'

'Papa's is the one closest to the house,' she murmured. 'Then Nita, then Miguel.'

The scrappy little hostler squinted at her. 'You sure about this?'

'I'm sure. I can't think of anyone I'd rather see have it.'

They lapsed into silence for a moment, tossing down the rest of their drinks and gazing at each other as if they were trying to etch the likeness of each of them in their minds.

'Well, then,' Jim said after a moment, 'what do you say we go find that Justice of the Peace?'

'I'd say I'm ready,' Corazón purred with a soft smile. 'Do I look all right?'

'You always look all right.'

He placed his hand at her waist, and nudged her toward the door.

'You guys coming?' he asked the others.

Doctor Morales just nodded at the invitation and started toward the door, behind Jonah Bennett.

That same schoolboy grin worked its way across Hoot Rafferty's weather-beaten face again and he pushed himself slowly up from the hard cane chair he'd flopped in.

'Wouldn't miss it for the world.'

10